TEST TIM

'Thank you, Fran

Gauvinier tried to put geniality into the words, but for the life of him he couldn't add 'Well bowled' to the captain's traditional dismissal of a bowler to his place among the fieldsmen. The scoreboard told the sorry story: 123 for one wicket, last man thirty-three. Billington were well on top, their two best batsmen in, playing well on a plumb wicket, and Tillingfold smarting from having to play with a substitute for their opening bowler. His boss had telephoned Gauvinier at twelve o'clock that morning to say that young Smith had been kicked by one of his horses and had had to be taken to the cottage hospital.

'Which arm?' inquired Gauvinier, before he could stop himself. It always seemed that his first thought was for Tillingfold Cricket Club . . .

Also by John Parker

TILLINGFOLD'S TOUR

TEST TIME AT TILLINGFOLD

John Parker

A STAR BOOK
published by
the Paperback Division of
W. H. ALLEN & Co. Plc

A Star Book
Published in 1987
by the Paperback Division of
W. H. Allen & Co. Plc
44 Hill Street, London W1X 8LB

First published in Great Britain
by Weidenfeld and Nicolson

Printed and bound in Great Britain by
Anchor Brendon Ltd, Tiptree, Essex

ISBN 0 352 31946 1

Chapter 1

'Thank you, Frank.'

Gauvinier tried to put geniality into the words, but for the life of him he couldn't add 'Well bowled' to the captain's traditional dismissal of a bowler to his place among the fieldsmen. The scoreboard told the sorry story: 123 for one wicket, last man thirty-three. Billington were well on top, their two best batsmen in, playing well on a plumb wicket, and Tillingfold smarting from having to play with a substitute for their opening bowler. His boss had telephoned Gauvinier at twelve o'clock that morning to say that young Smith had been kicked by one of his horses and had had to be taken to the cottage hospital.

'Which arm?' inquired Gauvinier, before he could stop himself. It always seemed that his first thought was for Tillingfold Cricket Club, and more human sentiments came later. 'Don't worry,' replied the metallic telephone voice which Gauvinier felt did not conceal the irony, 'Norman will be able to play for you next week. It's his left arm and nothing's broken.'

Now here were Tillingfold, up against it, and a bowler short.

He had already tried himself and Fred Bason; while Frank Hunter had just conceded forty runs in four overs. It was one of those days when Frank's leg-spinners either floated in as gentle full tosses or dropped amiably in to the pitch half-way along, just begging to be hit. 'The batsman is in two minds – whether to hit a four or a six,' Gauvinier thought grimly, spreading his fielders ever wider round the boundaries, so that a gently prodded shot could be an easily run one or even, to add insult to injury, a swiftly-taken two before Tillingfold's less agile sportsmen could reach the ball.

'Something's got to stop the rot.' Gauvinier, whose principle was always that a leader should lead, set the field for his own bowling. If anyone's average was to suffer it should be the captain's, he would tell his friend, Oliver Fanshawe, in their many discussions. Gauvinier bowled slow left-arm, but he didn't spin the ball very much. He relied more on subtleties of pace and flight and on a wicket which suited him could run through a side. On a batsman's paradise, like this one, the best he could do was to bowl a length and hope they wouldn't cane him too much. It would be a less difficult task, he thought, if he could rely on the wicket-keeper. Another drawback. His regular keeper, Joe Deacon, was away on holiday and young Trine, who had cheerfully volunteered to stand in behind the stumps, possessed a superfluity of confidence in his own abilities. Cheerfulness, thought Gauvinier, can make up for a lot, but not for four boundary byes, two dropped catches and a missed stumping.

He measured out his run. Just eight paces back from the crease, the last one a leaping stride and a half. He accepted the bowler's marker from the Billington umpire and pressed it into the ground with a firmness he did not feel.

'Left arm over, Jack.' The Billington umpire knew Gauvinier of old. If there was turn in the wicket, he would bowl 'round', running in at an angle with his easy pace, crossing in front of the umpire before delivering the ball. Bowling 'round' he increased the chance of l.b.w. decisions, and, if the fielders were awake, they could often pick up smart catches in the short leg positions. Today, although the sky was somewhat overcast, there was no swing in the light atmosphere, and his main hope was to pin the batsman down and to prevent Billington running away with the match.

He ran in on his curving run, his arm coming over high. Patterson, the batsman, moved his right leg back and across the wicket. The ball, pitching just short of a length and straightening ever so slightly with the left-hander's natural action, met the full face of a dead bat and rolled slowly back to Gauvinier. Patterson, who had already scored over fifty, thought: 'There's a hundred in this for me today' and settled at his crease to receive the next ball.

This time it was slightly shorter, and Patterson, stepping right across, hooked it off his body flat and square – to the chestnut trees for four, past the square-leg fielder who was some twenty yards in from the boundary. The stroke was inevitable and well-executed.

Gauvinier waved the fieldsman back to the boundary with some irritation. It was the third time he had told Mitterman to stay out on the boundary for this particular batsman. Mitterman, the club secretary-treasurer, was a poor fieldsman at the best of times, but usually Gauvinier managed to 'hide' him. On a day like this the batsmen seemed to seek out and find the weaknesses; and Mitterman compounded his dislike of five and a half ounces of hard leather coming at him at sixty miles an hour or more by an equal aversion to taking any hasty or violent action. In consequence, the only time he moved fast was in self-preservation, to avoid a ball struck straight at him; and his method of chasing the ball to the boundary was to set off after it at a measured trot which drove Gauvinier nearly to distraction. He also seemed not to appreciate the reason for fielding in any specific place, and found tedious the long walk between overs that fielding at square (or deep fine) leg entailed. Gauvinier was constantly chivvying his team to 'step it along, chaps' between the overs, and could hardly disguise his impatience. To minimize the cross-over, Mitterman would, from the third ball of an over onwards, edge his way infield, so that by the time 'over' was called he would have only a short walk to the other side of the wicket to take up his new position.

Gauvinier, acutely aware of his whole team while he was skippering, tried hard not to notice and to concentrate on bowling to a good length. Three balls brought no strokes and no runs. All right, so far. But as he turned to run in to deliver the last ball of the over he sensed, rather than saw, Mitterman at the square-leg umpire's elbow and edging in still further as Gauvinier began his run-up.

Annoyed, Gauvinier tried to bowl a much faster ball than usual. It pitched short and lifted a little, and Patterson clouted it as hard as he could towards the square-leg boundary. Because of the lift of the pitch he did not quite 'middle' it, and the ball soared high in the air before dropping a foot inside the boundary and going over for four runs. Had Mitterman been fielding where he had been told it would have dropped on his head, Gauvinier said bitterly later to Fanshawe. As it was, his skipper's exasperation boiled over. Gauvinier strode over to Mitterman and took him none too gently by the arm.

'Come with me, James,' he said, and walked the fielder to the boundary. At the spot where the ball had pitched, Gauvinier stopped, and turned Mitterman round.

'Here, James. This is where you should have been fielding. I'll give you something to help you remember.' And he took out of his pocket a 2p piece and placed it on the ground. 'There, you won't forget that, will you?'

Several small boys tittered, and one of the lounging onlookers laughed out loud. 'That'll learn 'im,' Gauvinier heard as he turned and ran back into the field for the next over. Mitterman, his face a study, walked deliberately across the wicket, holding up play for another long minute, while Gauvinier fumed ineffectually to himself in the slips. His temper was not improved by young Trine, standing up to the wicket, who looked back at him from under a raised arm and grinned cheerfully. 'Fifteen all, skip. Your serve.'

Bill Budgeon, who had been keeping one end going steadily but without any luck at all, put something extra into the first ball of his over, getting the ball to move away from the bat off the seam and lift appreciably. It flew off the outer edge of the bat, to Gauvinier's right, at waist height. Launching himself suddenly at it with instinctive reaction, Gauvinier reached a fraction too far. The ball thudded, not into the palm of his hand, but on to the ball of his right thumb. As he fell, outstretched, on the hard turf, the ball rolled slowly away for a single, and Gauvinier scrambled after it swearing to himself. The spectators and some of the field applauded sympathetically, and from somewhere a voice called out 'Well stopped, sir,' but Gauvinier knew he had dropped a catchable chance and was sick at heart.

As it happened, Patterson did not get his century. Facing Budgeon's next ball he suffered an unaccountable lapse of concentration and, jumping out to hit the ball clean over the bowler's head for six, checked his stroke and spooned it gently to mid-on, where Frank Hunter was pleased to redeem himself slightly by pocketing a simple catch.

'Wish they all came that easy,' he said beaming, as Gauvinier congratulated him and the bowler. 'That was a good try of yours.'

'Ah.' Gauvinier was still smarting. 'I should have had it, Frank. My mind was on other things.'

Hunter grinned cheerfully and glanced to the outfield, where Mitterman was carefully examining the daisies at his feet. With more tact than usual, he changed the subject.

'Look at what they've dug up this time. We're in for it.'

Billington, which was a small town but still considerably larger than the village of Tillingfold, had a name around this part of Sussex for attracting guest players of considerable merit. The incoming batsman, strolling casually to the wicket pulling on his batting gloves as he walked, looked as though he was born to the part. His flannels, once creamy white, wore that deeper tinge of yellow which comes of age and many washings. His boots had been cleaned, but the whitening was seamed across with countless cracks, like the old brown leather of his face. His bat was dark, battered and bound with tape. On his head he wore a faded cap, the orange and yellow circles of the MCC still faintly discernible.

'I see what you mean. I can't remember his name, but I'm sure I know him. Oh well.'

Gauvinier, instantly back deep in the game, made minor adjustments in the field placing, more for the sake of doing something than in any genuine hope of disturbing the new batsman. As that gentleman took guard and made his block with an experienced tap of the bat, a pale sun passed fleetingly across the wicket and Gauvinier, raising his eyes to the skies, put his trust in the strange game of cricket itself. The batsman settled and Budgeon rolled up to the wicket with his crab-like, shuffling gait, swung over his arm and delivered a slowish ball, perfectly straight and precisely on a length. Fluidly, the batsman's left leg went down the pitch, bat rock-like alongside it, a perfect forward defensive stroke. Somehow, however, the line was wrong and the ball, without deviating an inch, passed the reaching bat and gently, but irrevocably, removed the off-bail without disturbing the stumps.

Gauvinier and most of his team leapt in the air as one man. The batsman looked back once, unbelievingly, shook his head in mystification and set off for the pavilion.

'Well bowled. Well bowled, Bill. What a beauty.' The applause rang round the ground and in a twinkling 133 for one had become 133 for three on the scoreboard. Last man nothing, a golden duck, out first ball. Suddenly the wicket became possessed of devils, the fielding tightened, and the incoming batsmen faced a ring of grasping hands as eleven men sought hungrily to bring the magic hat-trick to the bowler.

The new man, young and irreverent, pulled the ball grotesquely from outside the off-stump round to square leg, missing Mitterman's outstretched hand and racing to the boundary in two bounces, shattering the atmosphere and restoring the batting side's dampened spirits. And Slater, the left-hander who had opened the batting and played a patient defensive role while Patterson was racing to his fifty, went over to the attack, hitting Gauvinier fluently for three fours and a two, all through the covers.

Worse was to come. By five o'clock Slater had moved to a well-deserved century and Billington declared at a massive 240 for six – a big score in an afternoon village match. Budgeon was Tillingfold's most successful bowler, with three wickets for ninety-seven runs; and Gauvinier claimed his only victim for seventy-nine runs with the last ball before tea when Slater was stranded half-way down the wicket attempting to clear the church spire. The batsman did not bother to look back for the stumping, merely continued the stroke as the start of his walk off the pitch. With 105 to his name he could afford to be generous, Gauvinier thought, clapping him ruefully into the pavilion.

'Well, it just wasn't our day,' Gauvinier remarked later that evening to Fanshawe, sitting in their favourite nook in the Dog and Duck. As so often happens when the luck is running against a side, nothing would go right for Tillingfold, and they had been dismissed for under 100 runs. Gauvinier himself scored eleven, being given out l.b.w. by the Billington umpire with his left leg (he was a right-handed batsman) stretched well down the wicket. It took all his conviction that cricket was more than a mere game to reach the pavilion without exploding; but by the time he banged through the dressing-room and slumped on to a locker, his mood had passed and he was ready to laugh at his own intensity.

'Sometimes I wish I could say "it's only a game", but I just can't,' he told Fanshawe. 'I get so enthusiastic and wrapped up in it I can't begin to realize that other people don't feel the same way. Then afterwards, like now, I look back at it all and wonder I could have made such a fool of myself.'

'It's what we all love you for so much.' Fanshawe had trod this path many times before. He felt a very deep affection for this man, whom he had known since they were children together in the halcyon days between the wars. 'Seriously, though, Peter, you went a bit far today. James isn't going to forgive you in a hurry.'

'I know. That's been on my mind even more than that blasted l.b.w. I get so mad with the man. He shouldn't be in the team at all, and yet we can't do without him. He's really put the club on its feet since he arrived in the village. It's one hell of a problem.'

They both pulled deeply at their beer, thinking of James Mitterman, chartered accountant and secretary-treasurer to Tillingfold Cricket Club. He had come to Tillingfold about five years before, a strange figure with the pale bland face of the later Noel Coward but lacking the charm and the wit. He and his wife Winifred had bought Little Standings, a Georgian house in its own grounds, on the outskirts of the village. They had furnished it with cool taste and, each in their own way, had set about becoming established in Tillingfold. There was no doubt about Mitterman's financial standing and yet Tillingfold, which had a way of winkling out other people's secrets, could make little of the pair. They knew that he had paid cash down for Little Standings at the height of the boom in the early seventies; those best informed said the price was nearer £50,000 than £40,000. They knew he drove a BMW which was renewed every two years; and they knew that he commuted to London four days a week, travelling first-class and paying over £700 a year for the privilege. They knew he had joined the cricket club and within a year had offered to become its secretary and treasurer, performing the joint duties punctiliously and well. In three years a £95 deficit had been transformed into a credit balance in the bank and no more did Gauvinier live in fear of what had happened one dreadful day in 1969 when, thanks to Frank Hunter's fixture arrangements, Tillingfold had travelled to Steynton to find no opponents awaiting them. Steynton had travelled to Tillingfold, where they found not the home side, but Beaubusson; so the two visiting clubs made the best of a bad job, playing each other on Tillingfold's wicket. As Gauvinier remarked at the time, it wouldn't have been so bad had they not also consumed

Tillingfold's excellent tea, and also (it had been raining and the square was quite soft) had made quite a mess of the pitch Tillingfold were saving for the important Raveley fixture the next week.

Tillingfold knew all this, but Mitterman was expert in avoiding the more pointed questions with which the local inquisitors tried to tax him. No one actually knew the name of his firm in the City; and although if pressed as to his origins he would murmur vaguely 'London', not even the most acute inquirer could discover anything about his past. Still 'it takes all sorts to make a world', as the old saying went, and most of the village interpreted this as meaning that if they did not know anything good about a man, they did not know anything bad about him either. So long as he was prepared to fall in with local ways, then he would be, if not accepted into the inner echelons of village society, at least tolerated. Fanshawe calculated that it took thirty years for a 'furriner' to gain complete acceptance, even in these modern permissive times. He would say to himself, in reassurance: 'It is the twentieth century, after all,' but sometimes he could hardly believe it.

While most inquiries withered for want of information where Mitterman himself was concerned, they were more successful with Winifred Mitterman. The lady, of the age indeterminate usually described as 'mid-thirties', had flaming red hair dressed in the style of Isadora Duncan as portrayed by Vanessa Redgrave, and her clothes were loose, flowing and made of the most expensive materials. The village had suspicions about her private life, but there was nothing anyone could place a finger on until she began to receive regular daytime visits from a youngish man with a beard, driving a Clubman Estate, with dark tinted windows, which prevented (maddeningly) the casual passer-by from peering in to see its contents. The mystery was solved a few months later when 'Portrait of a Naked Lady' formed most of that year's sensation at the Royal Academy. Gauvinier, confessing to himself the most vulgar curiosity, went to see it (several villagers took 'away-day' return tickets to London to do the same) and, being artistic himself, saw immediately what the furore was all about. The pose itself was demure enough, although the lady was undoubtedly naked, and equally undoubtedly Winifred Mitterman; the artist had captured such an expression of lust on the lady's face as to make it the most blatantly erotic painting Gauvinier had ever seen; more so than John at his most vulgar or Picasso at his most wanton. It inspired disapproving notices in *The Times* and the *Telegraph*, but two of the more popular dailies ran highly successful series entitled 'Pornography or Art?' and Winifred Mitterman turned down, it was said, vastly lucrative offers from *Playboy* and *Penthouse* magazines to provide them with what they both called 'centre spreads'.

In Tillingfold, and elsewhere, scandal does not die but goes to ground surprisingly quickly, to be disinterred from time to time as required. It was not long before the Mitterman Portrait ceased to be a regular topic of conversation. Nobody, of course, mentioned it to either James or Winifred, but curiously the episode, shocking though it undoubtedly was, made the pair somehow a little more acceptable to Tillingfold; as though the knowledge clothed the cold bones of the Mittermans with the flesh of reality. And after a discreet interval they recommenced their erosion of the ramparts of Tillingfold society, giving small cocktail parties and quiet dinners, while their guests tried in vain to discover in Winifred's violet eyes what the artist had found there and so blatantly exposed to public gaze.

Gauvinier took the two glasses and threaded his way through the throng at the bar for refills. The landlord, who was himself serving because of the Saturday night crush, saw him coming and had two pints of Sussex Special ready. It was really the blandest of all the real ales, thought Gauvinier, supping the 'head' off his pint to make carrying easier.

'Thanks, George,' he said to the landlord, passing over a pound note and waiting for his change. 'Busy tonight, then?'

'Not so bad, Peter. Hear you had a spot of bother today?'

'Yes, I suppose it's all around the village by now.'

'Sure to be. Must have been a bit of a laugh, leading him

around like a little boy and planting him in the right spot. He won't like it, you know.'

'He didn't. But I shouldn't have lost my temper. It's absurd, grown men behaving like that. I'll have to apologize to him, George.'

'Aye, you will that. But will he take it? I don't think you'll have an easy job there.' A clamour along the bar distracted him. 'All right, all right, I'm coming.' He added *sotto voce* to Gauvinier. 'Think they own the bloody pub, some of these youngsters. You mark my words, you take it easy with that Mitterman. I reckon he's a hard man.'

He nodded wisely to himself several times and lumbered heavily along the bar. So it was around already, thought Gauvinier. No doubt George Foster was right, at that. He'd have to find some way of apologizing to Mitterman for the sake of the club. He took his troubles, as so often before, back to Fanshawe along with the refilled pint glasses. Fanshawe was blunt with a friend's licence.

'If you'd done that to me, Peter, I'd have hit you back and all.' Fanshawe's cricketing days had been ended by a Messerschmitt shell exploding in the cockpit of his Hurricane. 'There's only one thing to do, and that's to apologize. Now. Don't leave it. If I were you I'd go round straight away and have it out with him. But don't read him a lecture on fielding if you want him to stay in the club.'

'I know, I know. Don't rub it in too hard. I'll just have to curb this blasted enthusiasm of mine somehow.'

He downed his beer in one long open-throated swallow.

'If only I could like the ruddy man.'

He always used 'ruddy' where 'bloody' was called for. It was a strange throwback to his upbringing. He lifted his hand to Fanshawe and backed out of the bar, dodging offers of refreshment on the way. His bicycle was leaning against the front wall of the pub and he pedalled slowly through Tillingfold, savouring the evening and trying to work out how he would approach Mitterman.

Little Standings stood well back from the road. Gauvinier free-wheeled silently round the circular tarmac drive, thinking how much more friendly was the crunch of gravel, leaned his cycle against the portico and pressed the doorbell. The plastic button was set in a sort of transparent illumination and soft chimes rang musically in thirds as he removed his finger. He grimaced slightly. The door was painted immaculately in cream, with a brass slot for letters fashionably low, at knee height. Gauvinier counted the dappled glass panes until a shadow moved against them, diffusing the light still further. Then he stepped back a short pace as the door opened and Mitterman stood there, holding a Turkish cigarette in an ivory holder between his first and second fingers, and resplendent in a plum-coloured brocaded garment loosely tied at the waist. Gauvinier's first inconsequential thought was: 'The only man in Britain who still wears a smoking jacket after dinner.'

He spoke quickly, slightly gruffly.

'James, I'm sorry to call at this hour, but I wanted to apologize for losing my temper this afternoon. It was inexcusable of me.' He felt resentful at the effort the little speech cost him. Mitterman smiled thinly.

'It's very good of you to take the trouble to come round at this hour.' He glanced at a heavy gold wristwatch. 'But you needn't have bothered. It isn't important.' His words were neither reception nor rejection of the apology. His manner gave no hint of anything more than resigned interest at such an inconvenient hour. Gauvinier felt even more like a chastened schoolboy. He recalled with startling clarity the evening forty years ago when he stood at this same step asking the then master of the house: 'Please sir, can I have my ball back?'

'It's just that I didn't want you to think it was anything personal.' Mitterman did not seem to have moved, but Gauvinier had the impression that he raised an eyebrow. 'I'm always forgetting that other people don't feel about cricket as I do. I get so intense about it. Childish, I know.' He laughed deprecatingly, hating himself. 'I wouldn't want anything I had done to harm the Club, you see.' Somehow he gave the word Club a capital C.

Mitterman smiled again. 'You have no need to worry, Peter. I may not be a first-class fieldsman, but at least I have the interests of the club at heart.' His capital C was just short of mimicry.

'Oh, good. I'm glad of that.' Gauvinier could think of nothing more to say. Had there been a hint of an accent on that second 'I'?

'That's good,' he said again awkwardly and turned to his bicycle. 'Goodnight, James.'

'One minute, Peter. I think this is yours.'

Mitterman held out a 2p piece.

Gauvinier mounted his machine with what dignity he could muster and rode back to the Dog and Duck, fuming. It was just before closing time, and he found Fanshawe waiting patiently. He looked up as Gauvinier strode in.

'How did it go? You don't look too happy.'

'Not happy? I should ruddy well think not. The bastard didn't even ask me in – I was forced to stand there on the doorstep making apologies like a grubby little urchin. He stood there puffing away at some foul-smelling cigarette and let me blather on. And then he had the cheek to suggest that he felt more for the club than I do. And he gave me my twopence back.'

'Was it as bad as that? At least he hasn't quit and left us in the lurch. But you'll obviously have to go easy with him in future. Don't look so down, old man. It's not the end of the world.'

Gauvinier laughed ruefully. 'I get so worked up about cricket and I know we need the blighter in the club. Being skipper isn't all beer and skittles you know. You have to be psychologist and Solomon all rolled into one. I really must pack it in this year. I've done my stint.'

'Don't be daft, Peter. You know you couldn't do that. Anyway, it's what we pay you for.'

He knew well that being captain of Tillingfold Cricket Club cost Gauvinier quite a considerable sum of money each year, not counting the time he put into the administration of the club, attending meetings, selecting teams, supervising net practice and keeping the club kit in order. To try to lighten some of the load on the skipper, he himself had managed to introduce a 'kitty' system for the drinks, whereby after a game every member of the team subscribed to a 'jug' which was passed round among both sides until it was empty. In addition, anyone who scored a fifty or took five wickets was expected to buy a 'jug' to celebrate his success. But at the Dog and Duck a 'jug' was a handsome pewter vessel of old-fashioned design, which took a full gallon, making success with Tillingfold an expensive business for young players like Paul White or Norman Smith. On many occasions he had seen Gauvinier's hand dip quietly into his pocket to make up the necessary sum, and he knew his friend would sooner shoot himself rather than dream of asking for anything back.

But there was another side to the coin, too. Fanshawe, whose family had lived in Tillingfold for upwards of twelve generations, knew the village and its occupants probably better than anyone alive, and he knew too the petty jealousies which developed and the damaging gossip. Someone like Gauvinier, who stood out from the ruck and was prepared to accept responsibility, would have to accept as well more than his fair share of the blame when things went wrong. The captain of Tillingfold Cricket Club might not have been the squire, nor the vicar, nor the doctor, but he still held rank in the village (even in the nineteen seventies) and in accepting the post he had to take the kicks as well as the ha'pence, as the Sussex saying went.

The object of such profound thoughts, who knew them just as well as his friend, laughed again, this time with genuine humour.

'God knows, I enjoy it. I sometimes think that being a village cricket captain is the most difficult job I've ever tackled. And then the next moment it's the easiest.'

He looked with affection at Fanshawe.

'For all your cynicism, there's not much you wouldn't do for the club either, and you know it, you old sod. Come on, I know it's after time, but I'll see if I can squeeze one for the road out of George.'

'It'll look good in the newspaper. "Cricket Captain drunk in charge of bicycle!" Did you see the fabulous Winifred?'

'Uh-uh.' Gauvinier, who loathed Americanisms, nevertheless used the all-purpose grunt. 'No such luck. But I think you're wrong there. She's a nice woman, for all the gossip. Come on, George, you can just manage another two halves, can't you?'

James Mitterman closed the front door of Little Standings and walked slowly back to the dining-room where his wife was drinking and discussing liqueurs with their guests. He felt confident and pleased with himself in the way he had handled the Gauvinier situation. The man had humiliated him in front of others and would have to pay for it. The small measure of revenge he had exacted on his front doorstep was only a down payment. Other instalments would surely follow. James Mitterman was not the type to be diminished in public. But he had a compartmentalized mind, which had closed its door on Gauvinier the moment the exchange was over. He advanced genially into the room. Really, he thought, Winifred could be a magnificent partner when she put her mind to it. She had a low threshhold of boredom, and quickly lost interest, but while a project was new, she could have few equals.

All he had told her was that he wanted to charm Brigadier-General Alexander Smyth in order to enlist the Brigadier's help in a little matter which might be of considerable benefit to 'my people in London'. He had told her nothing of the project, nor would do so, for he trusted no one, especially his wife. James Mitterman was not a crook, but he was a creature of his age, admirably equipped to deal with any eventuality in his chosen sphere of operation. In the City he was nearly as much of a mystery man as he was in Tillingfold. He was trained as an accountant, and was brilliant with figures; yet he did not hold an accountant's position. He was not a tycoon; yet he was on first-name terms with the waiters at the Connaught. He was not a property developer; but the rumour was that as other fortunes declined, so Mitterman prospered. He was not in shipping; yet he was a member at Lloyds. He was neither lawyer nor journalist; but he lunched frequently at the Wig and Pen. He was, perhaps, a hundred years behind his time, or, as he preferred to put it, a hundred years ahead of it. Cecil Rhodes would have recognized him, Andrew Carnegie would have used him. He was a middle-man, an entrepreneur. In the crude language of the nineteen seventies, James Mitterman was a fixer.

One part of Winifred Mitterman's mind was saying, Christ how boring, as she leaned across the table to accept a light from Alexander Smyth. Smyth did not stretch too far himself. He preferred to induce Winifred to bend her supple body towards him, to try to glimpse the breasts under the flowing material which seemed to reveal more than it concealed. He had been puzzling it out all the evening. Was his hostess, or was she not, wearing a brassière? It had become almost an obsession with him. He could not take his eyes off her. The flimsy silk at one moment admitted the possibility, at the next denied it. Alexander Smyth's manly instincts were aroused almost to the point of discomfort.

Phillippa Smyth, smiling ironically, accepted a Drambuie for herself and watched Winifred pour her husband a generous measure of Chivas Regal. She was twenty years younger than her husband, and knew him like a book. She rather pitied him. He was such an easy target for one so spectacular as Winifred Mitterman.

'Tell me, Winifred, if I may call you that—'

'Oh, please, we're going to be friends, I hope.'

'Yes indeed. Where did you get that spectacular material? You must have made your dress yourself. I've never seen anything like it.'

Winifred leaned back in her chair and sipped her crème de menthe before replying. Good, she thought, opposition. This thin dark woman looks as though she might be tough. She moved her shoulders as though embarrassed. Her nipples slid suggestively under the dress. Smyth's whisky stuck in his throat. He coughed.

'Oh, my husband picked it up from one of his oriental friends. I just ran it up from an old pattern. I've got some left. Would you like it?'

'No, no, I couldn't accept – I'm sure it wouldn't suit me. I've totally different colouring from yours . . .'

'Nonsense. I'll just see if I can find it.'

Mitterman intervened smoothly.

'Why don't you take Mrs Smyth – er, Phillippa – to look for it while we men take a cigar in the other room?' He turned to Smyth. 'That's one old-fashioned habit I like to maintain. What d'you think, sir?'

Smyth wrenched his attention from Winifred Mitterman's body back to her husband.

'What? Oh, yes. Excellent idea. But not too long, eh? Don't want the girls to think we're trying to drop them, what?'

He accepted a generous topping-up to his glass as the two women left the room together. Mitterman settled his guest in a comfortable armchair and came quickly to the object of the evening. He did not believe in unnecessary subtlety.

'Tell me, Brigadier, as a member of the county planning committee, what is your opinion of the law regarding the Green Belt areas?'

'Well, I suppose it's a necessary precaution. But it's a damned nuisance so far as any development is concerned. Why? Do you have anything specific in mind?' Smyth was no fool. He knew his subject, but wasn't giving anything away.

'No, nothing at the moment. But my partners in London are considering investment in this county and they've asked me to read myself in, as it were, to the situation. That's why I've invited you here tonight,' he added with disarming frankness.

'What d'you want to know about, then? It's all there in the Act to be read up.'

'Ah, but that's not the same as having an expert do it for you. Let me be frank. You've been a county councillor for some years now, most of them on the planning committee. You've taken a great interest and my contacts tell me you're regarded as one of the best men on the subject, certainly in this part of the world. My partners wonder if you would consider giving us a small part of your time – say one day a month – as a consultant and adviser. For a sufficient remuneration, of course.'

Brigadier Smyth considered. He was in the middle of his second term as county councillor, and at sixty-seven did not feel like standing again in eighteen months time. He'd been elected soon after retirement from the army on the wave of anti-labour sentiment which brought Heath to power in the early seventies and found public work a chore. His army pension had already been seriously eroded by inflation and although his children were off his hands and well-established in their own right, he found Phillippa, his second wife, quite an expensive luxury. He had no doubt that Mitterman and his colleagues would want something from him other than mere advice; but so far the proposition was completely legal and he had nothing to lose by exploring it.

'What do you mean by "sufficient remuneration"?'

'Should we say two hundred?'

Smyth wondered if he was hearing correctly.

'Two hundred? A month? A year?'

'Oh a day, of course. It might be more as the work progresses.'

'What work? I thought you had nothing immediate in mind.'

'Ah – my partners move very fast when they have made their decision. Oh – we pay in cash, of course. Is it a deal?'

'Why not? And may I say, thank you very much for thinking of me?'

'By no means. Our pleasure. And profit, we hope.' He looked at his watch. 'I think we have time for our first consultation now.' He produced a long white envelope from his pocket. 'I asked Winifred to keep Phillippa occupied for half an hour, and we have another fifteen minutes. Will that be all right with you?'

Smyth took the envelope and grinned.

'You're right when you said you move fast. But I must warn

you. Nothing illegal. I don't mind sailing close to the wind, but I'm not risking my reputation or my pension.'

'Nothing like that, I can assure you. Thank you for your frankness. It's merely a question of – using the rules correctly, and, of course, knowing which rules to use. Now, in the first place, how might one set about having the Green Belt regulations set aside?'

In her cream and green bedroom, Winifred Mitterman looked at her guest and grinned. To her surprise Phillippa saw it was a friendly one.

'I'm sorry,' said Winifred.

'Oh don't be. Alex is a born lecher. You didn't have to go to such lengths. At his age a glimpse of knee is enough for him to imagine himself half-way to the bedroom. What you were doing was like using a sledgehammer on a nut. But what's the big idea? What's it all about?'

'Haven't the faintest idea. James never tells me what his schemes are. He merely enlists my help when he thinks he needs it. Anyway, it was fun, and I've been a bit short on that for the past few months.'

'Have you sat for any good portraits recently? That's all Alexander's been talking of since we received your husband's invitation to dinner. The knowledge that he was going to meet someone who's set half London going around with its tongue hanging out has kept him going day and night. He takes you to bed with his pyjamas and puts you on with his Y-fronts in the morning. What was he like?'

Winifred followed the switch with no difficulty.

'My painter? Awful. He was like a car salesman – the build-up was marvellous but the model was faulty. He was super when he wanted to paint me; but that was all he really wanted to do. He got me so steamed up that I could have screamed – I think I did scream once or twice – but in bed it felt as though I was being stirred with a palette knife. Come to think of it, maybe I was.'

'Does your husband mind?'

'James has less passion in him than a fish finger. The only thing he cares about is money – money and prestige. But he's good at it. Whatever he's cooked up for your husband should be lucrative.'

'Hmmmm. That's all right, then. Alex finds my tastes too expensive, and some of his habits cost money as well. He wouldn't be averse to splashing a bit on you – he's quite generous when he fancies someone. If you can stand it, that is.'

'I must say he doesn't exactly make me want to leap between the sheets, if you'll forgive my saying so. But if James wants me to I shall take, shall we say, a friendly interest in what Alex has to offer. That's if you've no objection, of course.'

'Oh, don't mind me. But you'd better be warned. Alex thinks that two's a crowd, but three's company.'

'Oh hell, what a bore life is. Still, I suppose anything's better than doing nothing in this dead-and-alive hole. When he's made enough money I shall try to persuade James that we simply must have a place in town.'

'Mm. Lovely. But what would you do with it?'

Winifred walked deliberately across the room to the bed. Just as meticulously she arranged her limbs in the exact pose of the Academy portrait. She leaned forward, violet eyes fixed on Phillippa. For an instant, Phillippa felt bathed in sexuality, and then Winifred was on her feet again, back in her *gamine* role.

'Why should the men have all the fun? Come along, they must have finished their boring business by now. Let's pretend we're little ladies, after all.'

Chapter 2

Apart from the occasional rambling party and misplaced tourist, Tillingfold does not have many visitors. It is not a famous beauty spot, although its position under the lee of the South Downs is one of the most attractive in Sussex. Apart from one Roman ruin, partially excavated, there are no buildings of great antiquity. And Sir Mortimer Wheeler left the villa of Catullus Quintus Minimus only half exposed to the twentieth century because Fishbourne and Bignor, not many miles away, had archaeological splendours far more complete and elaborate. Some of the older cottages, by the nineteen seventies restored and refurbished to something better than pristine condition, had been dwellings since the fifteenth century, it is true, and 'Tylingfolde' can be found by the more diligent researcher in the county archives at Chichester. But there are no great country seats like Chatsworth, or even lesser baronial halls. Most of the larger houses in and around the village were once working farms, although 'Miller's' and 'Turner's Field' are names which have survived their original owner's occupations. Tillingfold does not have a river (although its muddy village pond is the source of a stream without a name that finds its way eventually into the Arun) so there is no trout to attract the angler, whether compleat or not. There are not even any large hotels, although some of the more imposing country houses have been converted over the years into 'rest centres' and 'health farms' where the rich and famous may slim at their leisure for £250 upwards a week. Apart from the rather garish red-brick council estate bordering the cricket field, and, of course, the roof-rash of television aerials, very little of the twentieth century might seem to have penetrated to Tillingfold.

There's nothing that can even be called industrialization, if you don't count the battery turkey farm and the Tillingfold Nurseries, with their acres of glass. Oh, and the mushroom factory, which provides work the year round for the village girls and quite a number of the women too, now that it's all right for a married woman to go out to work. Fifty pence an hour, and a forty-hour week. My, they could never do that in my young day. A pound a week as parlourmaid up at the big house, with the Colonel – no, not *our* Colonel, his father of course – liable to pinch your bottom as you were laying the table for breakfast. Ever such a fine gentleman he was, and cheeky too. They don't have the garden parties like they used to, with all the county parading on the lawns, and old Francis fussing and clacking like an old hen because the heels were ruining his grass. No, and the weather was always fine – always, you remember? for the Garden Party. And they had champagne in the big marquee and the dresses were that lovely. Oh, there's nothing like that these days. I don't know what the world's coming to. It's a common saying among the older Tillingfold folk.

And that was just what old Gran Smith was thinking as she sat in her window that summer's evening watching the clouds close in and waiting for the rain to break the dry spell. She was quite content in her old-fashioned window seat, from where she could see right down The Avenue, even without her glasses. She snorted. The Avenue, indeed. It used to be called Rosemary Lane, until a county councillor, a man of little humour, had moved into Little Standings opposite Gran's cottage. Whenever he wrote his address at the top of his deckle-edged notepaper he was reminded of the one joke that had survived his Victorian childhood and Presbyterian upbringing.

A new schoolteacher at the village school. The class was half empty. In came a little boy, dishevelled and panting.

'Johnny, why are you late?' demanded the teacher.

'Oh, Miss, I've been up Rosemary Lane.'

In comes another small boy. He's been running too.

'Well, Georgie, where have you been?'

'Up Rosemary Lane, Miss.'

'You too? Sit down, and don't be late again.'

A small girl comes in, and stands before the teacher, dimpling.

'I suppose you're going to tell me you've been up Rosemary Lane too?'

'Oh no, Miss. I am Rosemary Lane.'

It made the councillor shudder every time he wrote a letter. And one evening, furious, he flung down his pen and determined to put the matter right. It took him three years, but one triumphant day just before the Second World War, two council workmen unscrewed the neat signpost 'Rosemary Lane' and replaced it with 'The Avenue'. Forty years later, Gran Smith thought that the black on white paint still looked brash and new, and that 'The Avenue' sounded snobbish and would-be 'county'.

From her window, Gran watched Gauvinier's encounter with Mitterman on the doorstep of Little Standings. She could not, of course, hear what was said; but after seventy-five years experience of life she could tell a defeat from a victory at fifty yards, and the expression on Gauvinier's face as he pedalled away from the house told a story all in itself.

'He were that put out, Mr Gauvinier was,' she told her daughter-in-law the next day, when Mabel Smith called round with a punnet of raspberries for the old lady's tea. ''Course, that one' – she jerked her chin towards Little Standings, where Mitterman, unconscious of the surveillance, was carefully clipping dead-heads from his rosebushes – 'he thinks he's Lord

Muck, that one.' Which wasn't particularly fair on Mitterman, who was punctilious in his attentions to Gran, having fathomed from the beginning that she was a power in Tillingfold's little land.

Mabel, who was married to an ex-cricketer and whose son was the village's star bowler, knew all about the incident on the cricket field, and recounted it with some relish. Nobody really liked Mitterman or his wife, although nobody could find anything particular against them, except someone like Gran, who at seventy-five was entitled to make instant conclusions from her likes and dislikes.

'That Gauvinier, he wants to look out. 'Ten't no good rowing with the likes of he.' Gran jerked her chin again towards Mitterman, who was sweeping up a few strewn petals and placing them tidily in a wheelbarrow. 'He's a cold fish, that one.'

Her voice, like her eyes, was keen, and Mitterman looked up, as though he had heard himself being discussed, even through the glass of a window and at fifty yards range.

'Hush mother, he'll hear you.'

Gran chuckled.

''Twon't do him no good if he does, t'owd boogger,' she added, solely for the sake of shocking Mabel, whom she thought privately was a little stuck-up.

'Now, Mother, you mustn't use that sort of language. It isn't right.' Mabel was indignant.

'Don't you go tellin' me what I can and can't say, my gel. I say he's a boogger and that's what he is.' She paused and looked up at her daughter-in-law, standing square with her big-boned face flushed and righteous. 'Yes,' she added. 'He's a boogger – and a – a flusher.'

In spite of herself, Mabel laughed.

'A what?'

'A flusher,' said Gran firmly. 'Same as what they say on television.'

She was an inveterate fan of Westerns when she visited her son's house. She spurned possession of a television set for herself.

'Oh, you mean a four-flusher. A sort of crook?'

'That's right. That's what I said. A flusher.'

'Well, mother, you mustn't go around saying such things. Mr Mitterman could have the law on you. It's wicked.'

'Have the law on me? Not him. He dasn't go near the law.'

'Now mother, I won't have it. Mr Mitterman's a good, honest citizen like anyone else, and you're not to go around spreading tales about him. They're not true, and it isn't fair.'

'Fair's fair as makes fair.'

'Oh, go on with you, you wicked old woman.'

Gran cackled with laughter.

'You see if I'm not true,' was her parting shot as Mabel bustled away down The Avenue. 'Now, where's that milk? I likes a drop o' the milk with my raspberries.'

Across the road Mitterman, unconscious of the inspection and of the opinions expressed by the old lady, completed manicuring his roses, dropped the last thorny cutting in the wheelbarrow, removed his gardening gloves and wheeled the barrow carefully round the house to the compost heap. He had noticed the tiny flecks of greenfly beginning to spread on the buds, so he went to the garden shed and carefully mixed cartons of powdered insecticide into a garden spray. He donned a black plastic pair of trousers, a black plastic cape and a sou'wester. He tied a large white handkerchief over his mouth and nose and placed a large pair of sunglasses on his nose. Then, his hands encased in rubber gloves, he ventured forth to do battle with the greenfly. Winifred, seeing him from the drawing-room, came out holding a glass of sherry.

'You look like the man from Mars,' she told him.

He couldn't hear properly. He lifted the corner of the sou'-wester. 'I beg your pardon?'

'. . . the man from Mars.' Winifred raised her voice.

Mitterman smiled thinly and returned to the attack wielding his spray. Winifred, defeated by the stench, retired to the drawing-room. Her sherry didn't taste quite the same, she felt. When her husband came in, scrubbed and clean but with an aura of insecticide still clinging to his clothes, she asked him: 'Are all those precautions really necessary?'

'I always like to be completely prepared for any eventuality. If the instructions say the liquid must not be breathed, must be kept off the skin and off the clothes, and particularly out of the eyes, then I shall make sure those things do not happen.'

'Was that what you were doing last night? Making preparations?'

'In a different sense, yes of course I was. We hope to have every eventuality covered.'

'What's it all about, James? After all, I'm your bait, so I might as well know why you're hooking that particular fish.'

'All in good time, my dear. It should be very profitable.'

'I liked Phillippa. They won't get hurt, will they?'

'Good heavens, no. The worst they can hope to get out of this is several thousand pounds – tax free. With any luck we could all be quite rich.'

'What about Peter Gauvinier? What are your plans for him?'

'Oh, he's nothing to do with this scheme. He doesn't come into it. Forget him. He's not important.'

'Even after what he did to you on the cricket field yesterday? I know you, James. You wouldn't let something like that pass.'

'How did you know about that? I didn't mention it, and you haven't left the house.'

'I pay the milkman every Sunday, don't I? The whole village knows about it. And they're laughing,' she added, watching him closely.

Mitterman's mouth tightened.

'They'll be laughing on the other side of their faces if—'

'If what, James?'

'If nothing . . . Forget it, my dear. You're very inquisitive today.'

'Am I? Why shouldn't a wife know something about what her husband is doing?'

'No reason at all, my dear. Of course. But at the moment it's all very confidential.'

'You mean you can't trust me.' It was a statement, not a question.

'Not when there are several million pounds at stake. It wouldn't be fair on you.'

Winifred was impressed.

'That's a lot of money. All right. I'll be good. What do you want me to do next?'

'A small dinner party, I think – no, perhaps not. I don't want to do too much entertaining here.'

'For how many?'

'Oh, three or four.'

'Mixed?'

'No, I shouldn't think so. Possibly one woman. Three men, certainly.'

'Why don't we take them to Tyling Manor? That's discreet enough, if you don't want to advertise.'

'That will do very nicely.' He looked at her and smiled slightly. 'Sometimes, you can be most useful.'

'Thank you, kind sir, for the compliment.' But indeed it was a compliment, or as near as James Mitterman could come to delivering one. And on the following Wednesday night, James and Winifred Mitterman entertained Sir Philip Beeston and his secretary, Pauline Wilder, Fred Bason and Edward Trine to a very expensive meal at Tyling Manor, where they ate poached salmon and drank hock and talked far into the night. Winifred Mitterman, dancing in turns with the three male guests, thought she'd never been so bored in her life. But for ten per cent of, what was it? several millions, she was prepared to put up with it.

In Oliver Fanshawe, Tillingfold Cricket Club were fortunate in possessing one of those rare individuals who, while they seem to have no place in modern society, yet manage to survive and to find a niche where, apparently, no niche could possibly survive. Fanshawe's life had been divided into two parts at the age of twenty-three by the Messerschmitt shell. Before it, he had known joy and youthful enthusiasm and violent, almost hysterical action. An only child, he grew up in complete contrast to his moody but magnificently honest father, a writer who would compromise neither in fact nor fiction, and consequently eked out a meagre enough living. He had just enough to send his son to his old college. The young Oliver was a curious bundle of bouncing energy, hurtling through Cambridge like a meteor, one of the last genuine 'double-Blues' in cricket and rowing; and narrowly missing out on a Rugby Blue too. On his graduation day (Third Class Honours in Economics) he fled from Cambridge to London, walked into the first RAF recruiting station he came to, and signed up. The Second World War was three months away.

Fourteen months later Squadron Leader Fanshawe, awaiting a bar to his Distinguished Flying Cross, and with fourteen confirmed 'kills' to his credit, lay motionless in Upper Heyford hospital, the lower half of his body encased in plaster. He was drugged, enough to take the edge off the worst of the pain, but not enough to render him unconscious. The doctors clustered at the end of his bed; one older, with a clipped moustache and sharp black eyes; the others young, their faces as yet unformed so that he knew, even while lying there looking up at them, he would never remember them. They talked across him, about him, occasionally at him, but never to him. Even when they asked him a question, he felt dully, it was as if he was a piece of plasticine. 'Does *that* hurt?' 'Is *that* more comfortable?' Had he not been given those drugs, he thought, he would have screamed at them. 'This is *me*, not a wooden dummy. This is *me* who's never going to walk again. This is *me* who'll never be a father.' Only in the liquid eyes of the nurse could he find horror, pity, anything more than a professional interest in the plight of his body, or his mind. It was not until years afterwards that he began to appreciate that the nurses had to be like that. Personal involvement in the human debris of war would soon render their task intolerable.

Three days later they let Anne, his fiancée, in to see him. She sat by the bed holding his hand, tears streaming from her eyes.

He thought they looked like violets in the rain. She shook her head violently, back and forth, clutching at straws.

'They can't say that. They can't mean it. Darling – oh, darling – we'll put the wedding off for a few months. You'll get better. You must, you must—'

She collapsed forward, weeping into his hand. He could feel her face, warm and sticky with tears, her breath against the palm of his hand. He had no strength to withdraw it, or to bring his other hand across his body to caress her hair as he wished to. Through the pain and the drugs he suddenly saw, and as clear as a close-up photograph, the face of his father. The mouth did not speak, but the eyes looked at him with love, without pity. Dick Fanshawe had never shirked an issue, even his own cancer. His son knew what he had to do.

'Listen, Anne.' There were no endearments. Like the time for love, they were in the past.

'Listen to me. I'm finished. No, no, don't say anything, let me speak.'

His hand tightened around her face and forced it upwards so she had to look at him. His eyes were bleak, his face as hard as granite.

'You're to leave now, and don't come back. There's nothing left for us. I can't marry you, I can't give you children, and for the rest of my life, I'd be a burden on you. If I've anything left to give you, it is your freedom. Take it, and go, for my sake as well as yours.'

She couldn't speak. She collected her coat, and her gloves and her handbag, and walked out of the room without looking back. And Fanshawe, alone in the cold white ward, faced his future.

Strangely it was cricket which bridged the gap between his old life and his new cabbage existence. Twice a week, the green-uniformed ladies of the Women's Voluntary Service toured the wards, pushing a trolley on which were displayed sweets (rationing had started, but already the WVS were giving up their coupons for the wounded soldiers and airmen), fruit when it could be found, packs of cards, jigsaw puzzles and books. Among the more lurid titles Fanshawe spotted a familiar yellow cover, and made his first borrowing the first wartime edition of the cricketer's bible, Wisden's Almanac for 1940.

It was the year of the gathering storm, and in its usual unemotional style, Wisden told the remarkable story of the timeless Test that was never finished, when the England team abandoned its attempt to score more than 700 runs in the fourth innings to beat South Africa, and ran for the last boat home before war was declared. As if in defiance of the Nazi doctrine of racial purity, the West Indian Learie Constantine was the first of the traditional Five Cricketers of the Year. The others were Bill Edrich, Doug Wright, Brian Sellers and Walter Keaton. Fanshawe devoured the time-honoured features and thumbed idly through the volume. He read with interest the Wisden version of the University match, in which he had hardly distinguished himself with 0 and 22, and discovered that he had been fourth in the university averages for the season and was regarded as a coming batsman whose 'impetuosity should be curbed to allow for the development of a considerable natural talent'. Strange, it all seemed an age ago, as indeed it was, for him lying crippled in a hospital bed. Still, there would be little enough first-class cricket played in the next year or so. More for something to do to fill the idle hours, he began to comb the biographical edition of the Almanac, trying to discover how many university players had come through to play for England; and whether Oxford or Cambridge were predominant. He found that he could not make the calculation on the information available in one issue, and so he wrote to the Lord's librarian; and thus began an interest which rapidly grew into an obsession.

After a year, he was released from the hospital, and sent home to Tillingfold by a grateful government with a disability pension for life of £250 per annum, two medals with their striped ribbons in velvet-lined boxes, and a pair of aluminium crutches. He had made a remarkable recovery.

In truth, his body was young and very strong. The shattered pelvis soon mended, although the surgeons could never compensate adequately for the loss of a left hip-joint. More serious was the damage to the lower spine, but miraculously the motor nerves survived a terrible battering, and in time Fanshawe recovered at least partial use of both his legs. He would always walk with a pronounced limp, but he held his back as straight as a ramrod in defiance of fate; and he threw away his crutches after the war when he found that he could walk pushing a lawn mower up and down the Tillingfold pitch.

For his interest in cricket was not confined to the first-class game. He had spent many hundreds of hours researching in the archives for the history of Tillingfold Cricket Club. Over the years, a number of scholarly articles had appeared in the county *Times* and other local newspapers as he had uncovered a fact of particular local interest. But he had exhausted the resources of even the county archives in Chichester without ever plumbing his subject to its basic origins. The nearest he could discover was an old poster, advertising a match between 'Ye gentlemen of Billington and 15 Gentlemen of Tillingfold' in the year of Victoria's accession. There was no record that he could find extant of the result of the match, or any earlier reference to the foundation of the club. But he did not despair one day of discovering how cricket first came to Tillingfold, and when.

There were many in Tillingfold, particularly the younger generation, who thought Fanshawe a dry old stick. His upright, limping gait inspired many a youthful imitator, but if he noticed an occasional train of grubby infants trailing behind him along the village street, he paid no attention. Thanks to his degree, and his Cambridge connection, he found work on an occasional basis marking university board examinations, which brought him in a fair living to subsidize his pension and was of more use to him than a regular job; his injuries precluded conventional employment and he had no desire for a creative profession, like authorship. For many years he refused to drive, holding a deep conviction that cripples on the road were more prone to accidents than any other type of driver, but eventually improved techniques and a growing loathing of public transport persuaded him to invest in a little three-wheeled car with specially adapted controls. Behind the wheel of this dangerous-looking but no doubt perfectly safe form of conveyance, Oliver Fanshawe at approaching sixty miles an hour inspired in the residents of Tillingfold something of the fear he had instilled in the German pilots during the Battle of Britain. General opinion was that he was nearly as fast and twice as lethal.

His lifelong friend, confidant and mutual critic was Peter Gauvinier, twelve years younger. They shared the same abiding interest in cricket and total devotion to it at the village level. It was as though some of the young Fanshawe's love and enthusiasm had attached itself to Gauvinier to keep him eternally young.

'It's Peter Pan you should have been christened, not Peter Gauvinier,' Fanshawe would tell him. Yet, foolish as he knew he was, Gauvinier still could not rein his enthusiasm, even at forty-eight, for the game he loved and vowed he would until the day he died. And his enthusiasm was in no way diminished by a whole hatful of snubs he had received from others less dedicated through the years. 'Old Govineer,' they said in the village, 'he's gone crazy on that cricket of his.' And there was no doubt that, but for Gauvinier's enthusiasm and drive, and Fanshawe's love and insight, cricket would have died in Tillingfold after the war. Or, as Fanshawe put it, it would have been swallowed up by the all-devouring soccer.

Together they had rekindled the interest of Colonel Sir Edgar Trine, up at the Hall, and with some pre-war cricketers who had avoided having their names engraved on the granite column of the war memorial in the corner of the cricket field, they had built the club anew. In very much the same way as it had dwindled and nearly died after the First World War, so the cricket club faltered and then flourished again, part of the tradition of the village and, in the eyes of Gauvinier and Fanshawe and a few of their friends, possibly its most important part. They had to be careful not to express this sentiment out loud, for the human being is a very curious animal that often does not care to have its innermost feelings exposed to public view; and indeed may very well adopt the opposite public attitude to that which he holds deep within him, precisely so as to prevent prying eyes from discovering his secret. And nothing, as is well known, will frighten an Englishman off more quickly than a display of sentiment, unless of course it occurs on television or the films or on the stage, where you can wallow in it to your heart's content.

Somehow, however, cricket in Tillingfold had survived and had woven its way back into the fabric of village life. The popular folk tales of the sixties and seventies, the fortunes of the Archers and the goings-on in Coronation Street, were followed faithfully in Tillingfold as anywhere else in Britain; but in Tillingfold they'd know that these were fictional creations, for neither Ambridge nor the ubiquitous Street boasted a cricket club. And yet, astonishing though it may seem, not one in fifty of Tillingfold's males had ever held a cricket bat, let alone wielded one with serious intent.

All of which goes a small part of the way to explain how the battle of Tillingfold, as it became known at County Hall, came to be fought at all; and why it raised so much passion in so many breasts. But at this stage of the proceedings, the battle lines were only just being drawn, and only one person had any inkling that there would be a battle. And the person who sparked it off had no idea at all that he was doing so, and certainly no desire to do damage to anything or anyone, except perhaps in a very special sense to the attractive person of Miss Arabella Simpson, waitress and third daughter of Jack Simpson, Tillingfold's butcher.

For Norman Smith was in love with Arabella Simpson. And as Norman was seventeen years and eight months old, and all he had ever loved before was his mother and cricket, Norman was, as they put it in Sussex, in a right state. He just didn't know what to do about it, and it was affecting his whole life. His bowling, his batting, his relationships with his parents, even his job up at the stables seemed to be overshadowed by the huge and monstrous gloom which being in love seemed to inflict on Norman. Six foot three, broad-shouldered, and normally of a sunny if not too imaginative temperament, Norman Smith was reduced to an introspective mess at the very thought of the charms of Arabella. In the year before he had left Billington Grammar School, which was co-educational (prior to going comprehensive), Arabella had sat in the next desk to Norman in the Lower Fifth. For twelve whole months, he had sat less than three feet away from her, watching the swell of her breast as it thrust out the gingham of the school uniform, straining the buttons and revealing the occasional tantalizing glimpse of white. Sometimes, as she swung round in her seat, or flounced into it after break, he would catch a glimpse of leg above the knee; and one shameful day she had caught him looking and deliberately, he was sure, to mock him, she had flicked her skirt high as she settled it, showing him a long brown thigh and a delicious glimpse of matching knicker. He had not dared look for another three weeks in case he was caught again.

Modern novelists would have it that the permissive era in fact does permit everything, and that a lad of sixteen in Norman's position would, to put it crudely, 'have it made'. Yet permissiveness, as distinct from permission, seems reluctant to gain a foothold in the English countryside, and Tillingfold is no exception. And the truth of the matter was that, just as Norman had not spoken one word to Arabella for a full year while she was sitting next to him, other than to ask her if he could borrow her rubber/ink/pencil sharpener or whatever gambit he could think of, so too had Miss Simpson not actually addressed him voluntarily in all that time. And yet there was no doubt that both had been acutely aware of each other's presence.

Norman's job as stablehand at Harry Broome's Clinghammer Stables meant that most days he was 'mucking out' at dawn, and half an hour later was among a string of lads exercising the valuable thoroughbreds whose board, lodging and training cost their owners up to £100 a week. The spectacular ride took them up a spur of the Downs to the gallops along the top, and Norman loved the cool freshness of the summer mornings with the mists rolling down to the sea on one hand and England stretching away, apparently forever, to the north on the other. The track to the gallops led past Tyling Manor, now country club and the haunt of gourmets, where Arabella Simpson had taken a job as waitress after failing her CSE examinations. Norman had no idea that the princess he had admired from afar (two and a half feet) was living and working not a stone's throw from his own place of employment until one summer's morning she smiled up at him as he trotted his horse up the track and said: 'Hullo.'

Norman just managed not to fall off his horse from astonishment at seeing anyone, let alone a girl, there at five o'clock on a July morning. He did not even respond to her greeting.

'What – what the hell are you doing here at this hour?' he demanded, reining in his horse and turning it in the same movement, making her jump back. 'Sorry.'

'Well, that's the way to greet a body, I must say.'

Norman was only too conscious of her body, although it was dressed modestly enough. A high-necked white blouse peeped above a nurse's type of a cloak, and a mid-length skirt concealed more than it revealed of a pair of excellent legs.

'Oh – it's just that I didn't expect to see you there—'

'Where'd you expect to see me, then, Timbuctoo?' Miss Simpson was pert.

'No, I mean – yes, I mean—' Norman stumbled. Arabella laughed and took pity on him.

'No, you silly, I'm working there.' She jerked her thumb over her shoulder at the manor. 'And we've just had our monthly dinner-dance. It's just finished, I'm on my way home.'

'That's a bit late, isn't it? For a girl like you, I mean.'

'I don't know what you mean, a girl like me. You don't know what I'm like. You never paid me a moment's notice at that rotten old school.'

Norman's horse was becoming restless. It fretted and snorted, as if to remind its rider that it was not used to dalliance at five o'clock in the morning.

'Yes I did. I m – must be off.' Norman stuttered slightly in his earnestness. 'When – when's your day off?'

'Don't know as I'll get one this week—' she procrastinated.

Then, seeing the horse was about to take off in disgust, Norman or no Norman, she added hastily, 'Monday. Afternoon. See you at the Sunbeam. Two o'clock.'

Norman cantered up the hill track in a daze of happiness. His dream had come true; at five o'clock in the morning, Arabella Simpson had agreed to go out with him. Indeed, she'd even made the advance herself. He spent the next few days in a trance. Indeed, he was thinking of 'Bella when Morning Princess, no doubt jealous of his thoughts, caught him a fearful thwack on the elbow with her near hind hoof, putting him out of action for ten days and costing him a county trial. When they met at the Sunbeam café in the High Street on the following Monday afternoon, nothing seemed to go right. For Norman, it was the beginning of something like a nightmare. In the first place, they had to wait more than thirty-five minutes for a bus to take them into Billington. The buses actually ran every half an hour, but due to shortage of drivers the company was often forced to cancel a service or two each day. So Norman and Arabella had to wait, and then to stand, hot and sticky, for the half-hour rambling journey, jolting through the lanes. Then the X-film advertised had not arrived, so they were obliged to settle for an old AA which they'd both seen before; and as they were entering the foyer there was much giggling from three of their former school friends who seemed to be queuing up to poke fun at them. Once safely in the cinema, Norman tried, greatly daring, to hold Arabella's hand, but she soon told him it was too hot and sweaty, and she wouldn't let him put his arm around her. 'People will see,' she hissed at him.

It was the same next time, and the time after that. Norman seemed to feel all fingers and thumbs when Arabella was near. He flushed, floundered and fumbled. And the worse it became, the more deeply he loved her. He longed to hold her, to cosset her, to kiss her. In his secret heart he longed to touch her and do all those secret things he'd read about in the magazines. But to him she was so precious, so beautiful, that he would sooner drop a piece of Dresden china than harm a hair on her head.

His condition did not pass unnoticed, but he spurned offers of help and advice. His father had never been at ease with him since he'd taken an independent line and insisted on leaving school the previous year; while his mother was too inarticulate, or too wise, to try to sympathize. So, after something of a struggle with himself, he did what he'd been accustomed to do ever since he was a small boy. He went along to his grandmother for what she used to term 'a little chat'. There was something about Gran, thought Norman, that never let you down.

Old Mrs Smith saw him coming up 'The Avenue', head low, and smiled to herself. She liked Norman. He was honest and straightforward; above all he was generous. She did not like mean men, and she had always felt her son, Norman's father who ran the grocery shop, had been mean. True, he'd been brought up amid the fearful privations of the twenties and thirties, when she'd been forced by pregnancy to leave her smart job as chambermaid up at the Hall and manage on Syd's wages as a labourer. Maybe, she sighed to herself, maybe if things had been different. But her son had made a success after all, even if Syd hadn't; and now Norman was just starting. He'd do well. He was big, and people liked big men. However, here he was, holding his cap in his hands and turning it over and over. To be sure, it was a gentleman's riding hat, not like the cloth cap of her Syd's, but in the action she saw again the husband of fifty years ago.

'Come in, then, young Norman, and make me a cup o' tea,' she said briskly. 'You can tell me what you want while you're setting the tray. I know you want something. You only come to me when you do.'

Norman grinned. He was at ease already. He knew his grandmother. She never beat about the bush when she could poke her stick straight into it. He blushed slightly, and hesitated.

'It's a girl. I knew it. Moment I see'd ye comin' up the lane, I knew it.' She crowed. 'Well, not before time.' She grabbed his arm. 'Who is she then? Who is the minx?'

Shyly, he stumbled out his story. His hopes, his fears and his frustrations lay before them on the little table between the teacups. On occasions like this, her Sussex brogue lay heavy on her tongue.

'You'm blind, boy. That one, she's been after you a twelvemonth since. I know her, Simpson, butcher's daughter. She's that dark hussy with the curls and blue eyes. You want to marry her?'

He nodded, not trusting himself to speak.

'You be fool, boy. You'm too young to marry yet.' She cackled. 'Better you get her into bed, get it out of your system.'

Norman protested, blushing. 'Oh, come on, Gran, you mustn't. It isn't like that.'

'Nonsense. Course it is. An a dang good job too, else we wouldn't be here now.'

'Oh Gran, we couldn't. Anyway, she won't let me touch her.'

'Oh, so that's the way the land lies. Both of you sniffin' around like a dog and a bitch on heat, and both of you too frightened to spit? Garn, don't know what things is coming to these days. 'Tweren't like that in my day.'

Norman was shocked to the core. He threw up his hands.

'Oh get away, Gran, how can you talk like that? You were old-fashioned then.'

'Wouldn't hurt you to get old-fashioned, then.' She mimicked him. 'S'pose you want to fly to Spain, or one of them islands. What you been doin' with this 'Bella then? Spendin' good money on films, an' ice-creams, and fish and chips, and such? And chocolates?'

'Well—'

'I thought so. All the young folk want to do these days, is spend money. You don't need to spend money on lovin'. That's daft. It comes free, you set about it the right way.'

Norman wondered if the old lady had been drinking.

''Tes right, my boy. Never pay fur lovin'. You'll pay for it in the end, so you don't want to pay for it to start with.' She cackled again. 'Look boy, 'tes summer, en' it?' Norman nodded.

'You want to get your girl into bed? Then tek her into a bed o' hay. Tek her up hayfield and lay her down on hay, then. 'Tis the softest bed you'll ever find.'

Her cackle stilled and the old lady's eyes dimmed. She was fifty years away, the trim parlourmaid in her black dress and white apron, slipping out of the Hall on a hot drowsy afternoon, to the field where her Syd, stripped to the waist, red-brown in the sun and his muscles rippling, laid down his scythe and took her in his arms; and the smell of the newly mown hay, the smell of him, the warmth and smoothness of him, the strength of his arms, the taste of the salt sweat on his lips sent tremors clean through her body, and her limbs turned to water and he laid her gently, so gently for a big man, on the soft hay . . .

Her eyes opened and she smiled radiantly at her grandson. 'Take her in the hay, boy. Take her in the hay.' She looked all of seventeen.

Norman, scandalized, bid a hasty farewell and departed before her memories became any more explicit. He was shocked, but excited. Old Gran, she knew a thing or two, he reckoned. She certainly did.

That afternoon, when they'd had their cup of coffee at the Sunbeam, instead of turning right out of the café towards the bus-stop, he grasped Arabella's arm firmly and turned her left towards the road that led to the Downs.

'Where are you taking me?' demanded Arabella, to whom such masterful behaviour was a strange, albeit welcome, departure from the usual.

'I thought we'd just go for a walk. Not very far.'

Arabella complained that she wasn't dressed for walking, and indeed her new platform shoes, which brought the top of her curly dark head just level with Norman's chin, were not the most suitable for a country stroll. But she rather liked this new decisive Norman, and she made little fuss. He was delighted with his initial success, while she knew she'd easily be able to control him even if his ardour did manage to overcome his shyness. She covered any slight nervousness she might be feeling with a flow of inconsequential chatter as they strolled together, not touching, up the long slope into the foothills of the Downs.

''Course my friend Nellie 'n me are going to the dance on Friday. Pity you don't like dancin', Norm. At the Starlight Room, you know. They're getting one of those pop stars from London down, and a big group, the Jujubes. It'll be ever so nice. I like that guitarist, he makes me go all goosy inside.

'Is that Jess who plays for the cricket club the Albert Jess who used to lead the Money Spinners? Is it really? He looks ever so old, close to. I used to think he was super. I've got all his records. Has he stopped making them now? What does he do? I s'pose he's made ever so much money. Wonder why he comes and lives in a dump like this. If I had his money I'd go and live in Bermuda, or Ibiza, or somewhere.'

Arabella had once been on a package holiday to Majorca, and Ibiza was to her the height of luxury.

'All right, I know you don't know. I was only talking, wasn't I? It's not much fun, when a girl has to do all the talking.'

'Go on, I like it. I'm thinking.' In truth, Norman had hardly heard a word. His mind was occupied with his strategy. He wondered how he was ever going to persuade her to climb the gate into the hayfield wearing those shoes. That skirt would be a nuisance too, half-way down her shins. And she wouldn't want to get that blouse dirty. Though it *was* flimsy. He could see the outline of her—

'What are you looking at me like that for?' Arabella demanded sharply. 'I don't reckon you're up to much good, Master Norman Smith. Phew, it's hot walking up this old lane.' She fanned herself with her hand. Norman seized his chance.

'There's a place in a minute where we can sit down in the shade and have a rest,' he said ingenuously, adding, deliberately misinterpreting her cautious look: 'Don't worry, there aren't any cowpats – or any cows.'

''Ten't animals with four legs I be feared of,' said Arabella, lapsing into brogue, but grinning at him. ''Tes two-legged sort.'

Norman blushed.

'Oh come on, 'Bella. I wasn't thinking anything of the sort.'

'What sort?'

'You know, that sort of thing.'

'What sort of thing?'

It appeared to be one of those conversations which has no end, and Norman was grateful that they had arrived at the gate into the newly mown hayfield. She wouldn't go into the field, but climbed with scant regard to her clothes on to the five-barred gate, and sat swinging her legs. She patted the top rail next to her, and he clambered up and sat beside her, wondering how to make the next move. Arabella chattered on.

'Ever such a late night last Wednesday. That Mitterman gave a dinner party, and they went on dancing till after two. I don't like him. He's a smooth one, all my dears and never meaning it. Had me running backward and forward from the kitchen all night, and only a fiftypence tip at the end. Mean old sod, but he was lashing it out. Cost him more than £50. Mr Edward was there too. He's a right one. Can't keep his hands to himself. He put his hand right up – made me jump and I spilt his melon down his front. Serve him right. But he's rather nice, doesn't really mean anything. You know. They was talking ever such a long time. Something about the cricket field. Mrs Mitterman looked bored most of the time, having to dance with Sir whatever-his-name-was. I bet she's a handful for old Mitterman. She and Mr Edward did a fancy tango and he was throwing her all over the place, showing her knickers, the lot. Old Mitterman didn't seem to notice. Too busy talking, he was. Norman, you're not listening to me. Norman!'

He'd dropped off the gate into the field and stood leaning with his back to it. The field curved away over the horizon, hazy in the warm sunshine, the rows of ripening hay spreading away into the distance, golden waves breaking on a green beach. Already they were turning honey-coloured. There were splashes of yellow buttercup among the mown green grass, and the air was murmurous with bees and moving with butterflies. He did not answer her. He turned, grasped her firmly round the waist and lifted her effortlessly off the gate.

Her legs kicked out in a whirl of red skirt and white petticoat as she gasped and fought. Her shoes fell off, unnoticed.

'Norman. Put me down. You beast. Norman. Put me down. I'll – Norman!'

'I'll put you down, if you promise to stop kicking.'

He carried her into the field, alongside the thick hedge bordering the lane. The curve of the field meant they were totally out of sight of the road.

'Put me down Norman! *Put me down.* I'll scream . . .'

'Scream all you want, 'Bella. I'm not hurting you. No one can hear you.'

She capitulated.

'All right, you big bully. Put me down. I can't fight you, you're too big.'

Tenderly he set her on her feet, gently kissing the back of her neck as he did so. Immediately he was gasping as her elbow caught him in the stomach and she was away, running barefoot over the swathes of hay. Swearing, he set off in pursuit, not noticing that she took care not to run for the safety of the gate but drawing further and deeper into the field. Suddenly she tripped as he reached for her and went down, head first into the soft hay, and in an instant he was down beside her and they were lying panting, looking up at the blue sky and laughing together. He held her hand and watched the rise and fall of her breast.

''Bella . . .' His voice was low, questioning.

'Mmmmh?' Hers was content, teasing.

'Why d'you run away?'

'Why d'you think?' Turning blue eyes full on him.

He turned on one elbow, looking down at her. Her black hair tumbled about her face, framing it in curls. Her eyes were bluer than the cornflowers growing in the field. There was a tiny beading of sweat on her forehead and her face was still flushed from the chase. He watched the straight line of the nose wrinkle familiarly at him and the red lips open under his gaze to show pearly white teeth and the tip of a pink tongue, gleaming with moisture. Almost without his knowledge his hand moved up along her side to her breast, which heaved deeply, twice, as though she could not control her emotion. He heard her breath catch, and her body trembled under his hands. Keeping his eyes fixed on hers, he bent down to kiss her, and as he did so saw two great tears well up and spill from her eyes down her cheeks. He checked, and she sat up swiftly, thrusting him from her and emitting the most violently explosive sneeze he had ever heard.

One sneeze followed another and he sat dumbfounded and helpless as the paroxysms rocked her body. A hand fluttered out towards him and he seized it only to be thrust away. From behind her hands covering her face he caught a strangled gasp.

'Hanky—'

He produced a crumpled – none too clean – handkerchief from his pocket and Arabella, not caring whether it was white or black, mopped at her streaming face. Eventually she gained control and the sneezing died down to an occasional sniff. She looked through blotched skin and red-rimmed eyes at Norman. She managed a smile.

'Sorry – couldn't help it – hay fever. We'd better go.'

Norman controlled his disappointment to the best of his ability, and escorted her tenderly from the field. By the time they reached the Sunbeam once more, Arabella was more or less restored to normal, and Norman resigned to try again another day. She grinned at him.

'Well, it saved me from a fate worse than death.' And was instantly contrite. 'No, I didn't mean that. I'll make it up to you.'

She pulled his head down to her level and said: 'Let me whisper.'

Norman inclined his ear to her. Instantly she stuck her tongue in it and worked it round, breaking away laughing as he shied back. But Norman was learning.

'Is that a promise?' he asked quizzically.

'No,' said Arabella. 'A threat.'

And together they entered the Sunbeam, knowing a great deal more about each other than they had an hour before. That evening, when Norman called round to see his grandmother on the way to nets, she laughed and laughed until he feared for her health.

'But it worked, Gran,' he insisted. 'In spite of the hay fever. I really am going to marry her. Next year.'

He smiled at her and picked up his cricket bag. She stared after his retreating back. He'd be eighteen in two months time, a man. He'd have the vote. It was the age at which his father, her son, had strode off down the lane on his way to enlist for the Second German war. They didn't really get younger all the time, they just seemed to. Gran Smith chuckled to herself. Hay fever indeed. There was a young madam that needed a good talking to. If she was my daughter, I'd . . . But she's not. And it certainly sounded as if she could look after herself, if not for long. Gran remembered Norman's grandfather. *She* had thought that *she* could hold out against him, but she hadn't. And, apart from those few years, she'd never regretted it. She poured herself out a sherry. It was an evening for celebration.

'Mary Smith, you're a wicked old woman,' she said to herself and chuckled.

She settled in her window seat and opened *Pride and Prejudice.* On these long summer evenings she could read and at the same time keep an eye on the village. The book was leatherbound, and very worn. She knew every one of its 400 pages; it was an old friend. And yet she could always find something new in it to delight and distract her, just as she could find entertainment and variety in the village of Tillingfold itself. She had no need of television. As she would tell her cronies, 'It's no good being old if you don't enjoy yourself.'

Chapter 3

At the start of each season, when the players were at their most keen and eager to get into the side, nets were arranged at Tillingfold every Monday and Thursday evening. But later on, when the team settled down and the fair weather cricketers, as Gauvinier called them, began to find excuses for not turning up more often than was strictly necessary, even Gauvinier agreed that it was wiser to cut it down to one practice a week. Even so, sometimes after the beginning of July not more than four or five of the genuinely enthusiastic players would turn out for nets regularly unless there was competition for a big match like the annual Raveley fixture.

The evening of the day that young Norman Smith made his first unsuccessful attempt to seduce Arabella Simpson, was particularly memorable for Peter Gauvinier. In the first place, Norman, bowling with a fire and pace he'd never shown before (working off his frustrations), got his third ball to rear and laid Gauvinier out with a glancing blow to the temple. In the second, James Mitterman not only attended practice but apologized to Gauvinier for his behaviour the previous Saturday night. And thirdly, Gauvinier received his first hint of the struggle that lay ahead for Tillingfold Cricket Club, although he did not realize it at the time.

At first, all he could recall of the stunning blow to the side of his face was the curious slow-motion sensation he had when falling. When he opened his eyes the players were clustered around him and Norman Smith was bending over him, chalk-white with fright.

'Are you all right, Mr Gauvinier? Are you all right?'

Haynes had run into the pavilion and brought back a dirty towel soaked in cold water. Gauvinier pushed away the sympathetic hands and held the towel to his temple as he sat up. It came away stained bright with blood, he noticed with some surprise. His teeth ached, more than anything else. He felt slightly sick, but he waved the sympathizers back. He could not bear a fuss.

Somebody picked up his bat, somebody else his cap; and yet a third helped him to his feet and half-led, half-carried him round to the side of the net. He thanked them and insisted they carry on with the practice.

'I'll be all right. I'll be OK. Don't worry about me. It's nothing. Don't fuss, please. I'll be fine. I'll just sit here and recover.' He shooed them back to the nets with his hands. Norman, who felt guilty, stayed with him and helped him off with his pads. He really did feel fine, just a little giddy, and as soon as the blood was staunched he began to tidy up the gear. Pads and gloves were strewn around the big club bag, and he took the opportunity to sort them out into pairs, and to give the old bag a good shake-out.

'I've been wanting to do that for some time, so it's an ill wind,' he told Norman. 'You go and sling down a few more. Don't let a little thing like this put you off. It was my fault. That's what the Lord gave man a bat for. I'll be right as rain in the morning. Off you go. I want to see more of that pace. I always knew you'd got it in you.'

Norman without a cricket ball in his hand had few aggressive intentions. In his relief that Gauvinier was not badly hurt he tried to change the subject of conversation, wrenching it away from the object of one embarrassment to another.

'They were talking about the cricket club the other night up at the Manor,' he said abruptly.

'Who were? What were they saying?' Gauvinier recognized the lad's eagerness to make amends.

'Oh, Mr Mitterman and some people. Mr Trine was there. My girl—' (he used the phrase unconsciously but with pride and the poet in Gauvinier instantly recognized the world of meaning it contained) 'my girl heard them talking. Mr Trine tried to get fresh. He'd better not do anything like that again.' Norman's brows lowered.

'What were they talking about?' Gauvinier liked to know what others were saying about the club. Sometimes it felt as if it were really *his* club.

'Oh, I don't know. I don't think 'Bella knows anything about cricket. She was waiting at their table. Not that she listened,' he added hastily. 'She couldn't help hearing the words cricket club and she knew I'd be interested.'

'Oh, well, it's probably just gossip.' He was thinking of Mitterman and the row over the fielding; although he doubted whether Mitterman would have raised that subject himself.

'No, I don't think so, Mr Gauvinier. They were talking about it ever so late. They went on a long time.'

'Thanks, Norman. Maybe it's something we ought to know about.' But he did not feel like approaching Mitterman, who came up at that moment to don his pads for a knock. As he was adjusting the straps, Mitterman asked him sympathetically how he was feeling.

'That was a very nasty knock, Peter. Very nasty indeed. Don't you think you should go and see Doctor Emberton? Just to make sure, I mean, there's no damage.'

'Oh lord, it was only a bang on the head.' Gauvinier laughed. 'It's about the only place that couldn't do me any harm at all. I'll be right as rain tomorrow, except for a headache.'

'I hope so,' Mitterman was dubious. 'Do you feel up to a session on the accounts after practice?'

Gauvinier took this as an olive branch.

'Provided we can do it in the Dog and Duck and I can buy you a beer, James.'

Mitterman smiled.

'All right, but you must let me buy the beer. I owe you an apology.'

Gauvinier, instantly embarrassed, laughed it off. But he still felt sufficiently ill at ease with Mitterman not to want to raise the subject of the dinner at the Manor. It would look, his sensitive antennae told him, as though he were spying, and he kept strictly away from the subject during their short talk in the pub.

They sat together in the back parlour of the Dog and Duck, which had in centuries past been a skittle alley. When the brewery had modernized the public house, some twenty years before, George Butler, the landlord, had with some ingenuity scoured the country and, near Birmingham, had found a genuine old skittle table, leather sides, back, netting and all. Now for miles around teams came to play the Dog and Duck experts, hurling the wooden ball across the room. Grundy's at Bridport had provided the safety netting to order, the same mesh and strength used for the Centre Court at Wimbledon. Occasionally an over-enthusiastic throw would send a ball or a skittle clattering round the room to the grave risk of customers and their glasses, but by some miracle there had never been a serious injury even on packed club nights, and the Dog and Duck had profited greatly by this journey into the past. The modernization of the rest of the inn had left the little back room untouched, and Gauvinier preferred its bare whitewashed walls and old wooden tables and benches to the plush wall seats, horse brasses and subdued lighting of the 'saloon' and the plastic surfaces and juke box of the 'public'.

Tonight, for once, nobody was playing, and they were able to converse without the clackety-clack of the skittles. Mitterman was concerned with the future.

'The club is heading straight for trouble, Peter.' He emphasized each point with a dab of his forefinger on the accounts books. It was a habit which infuriated Gauvinier, who wanted to pick his nose in retaliation, and then banished the temptation as childish and unworthy.

'Look. We have £200 in the bank, but no assets worth speaking of at all. We get through five bats a year, and that's £150 at least now. The club needs a new bag; and there are at least three pairs of pads that must be repaired if not replaced before next season. Joe Deacon was muttering about a second pair of wicketkeeper's gloves, and the big mower needs a complete overhaul. Frank Hunter will do it, but even he will charge us £50. You know the square is breaking up. It needs re-laying professionally. And that'll cost us at least a thousand pounds. And on top of that the Parish is bound to increase the ground rent next year – they've kept it down to £100 for the past five years but it's bound to double this year, at least. We've got twenty-three members paying the full subscription of £5 and ten youngsters at a pound a head. To my mind that's expenditure of at least £1,500 within the next twelve months and a guaranteed income of . . . let's see . . . £230 including the vice-presidents' subscriptions. The figures just don't make sense.'

'They make a darned sight more sense than they did four years ago, James.' Gauvinier was eternally grateful to Mitterman's financial expertise but did not share his forebodings.

'In those days we were lucky not to be £200 in the red. It was only thanks to Charles Spinks that the club didn't close down years ago,' he said cheerfully. 'I agree we need the kit renewed, and the square will have to be done some time. But the turf's been wearing thin ever since I've known it and it hasn't disappeared yet, and the parish council hasn't foreclosed on us yet either. And while Trine's there I'm sure they never will.'

'I wouldn't be so sure of that, Peter,' said Mitterman darkly. He shrugged. 'But perhaps you're right. But all these things have to be considered. In my opinion we should set up a trust to buy our own land for the club. I'm sure there's enough goodwill in this district to subscribe to that.

'Imagine it.' His voice took on an uncharacteristic warmth. 'Tillingfold Cricket Club, after all these years, with a ground of its own. Its own pavilion, its own amenities. No more squabbles with the football team. No more graffiti in those dreadful toilets.' He shuddered. Gauvinier grinned at him.

'It's a nice thought James, but who's dreaming now? You've always accused me of having my head in the clouds as far as the club is concerned. In any case, I'm not so sure I'd like to see cricket leave the field after all these years. It's more than 140 now, you know, as far as Oliver can make it out.'

'You never know, Peter. You never know. Ways and means can be found.'

Mitterman drank his half-pint of lager and departed, leaving Gauvinier staring after him in astonishment.

'Now what was all that about?' he thought. 'Just what is he playing at?' And immediately put the uncharacteristic behaviour of James Mitterman out of his mind.

The next day was his 'London' day. As the senior copywriter for a leading advertising agency, for some years now he had been able to do much of his work at home, with weekly visits to the office overlooking St Paul's and periodic consultations over inordinately long lunches with his richer clients. Most of the week he spent at his roll-top desk (a legacy from his father) in the little room he and Polly had turned into his study. His London colleagues regarded him an eccentric rustic, an impression he did his best to promote, with whims that must be tolerated for his intermittent bursts of brilliance. Gauvinier was no fool. He did not conceal from himself that he worked hard enough merely to keep the bosses off his back; and that this was possible because he was able to look up from his desk and see green grass and hedges. He also found he was able to do three times the amount of work at home that he did in London. Put another way, he did as much work as he had done in London in one-third of the time. He saved money on fares and his blood pressure remained constant. Every Friday he delivered a week's output to his secretary and answered those letters he didn't throw into the wastepaper basket.

As usual, he was still overfull from lunchtime and listless as he stepped off the train at seven o'clock that evening, irritated and bored because he had completed his crossword on the way up to town in the morning and had been unable, due to a strike, to obtain an evening paper for the return journey. But the fresh breeze blew the showers into his face as he walked the few hundred yards to Billington Hospital, where Polly was just finishing her stint as ward sister. She'd gone back to nursing once Michael and Jill were off her hands. She kissed him briskly and hustled him into the car.

'I've got to hurry tonight. We're rehearsing.' Polly was a stalwart member of the Tillingfold Amateur Dramatic Society, whose production of *Night Must Fall* was due to be staged at the village hall in a fortnight's time. 'Oh and by the way, Mrs Veyzey wants to see you. She said it was urgent. You'd better give her a call when you've had something to eat. She's inclined to panic, so it's probably not as vital as all that.'

Gauvinier wondered what the vicar's wife could want. She was an earnest, rather formidable lady somewhat older than her husband, who was large and amiable and fond of real beer. He had been a fair cricketer in his time too, but a ruptured cartilage and some heavy-handed surgery had put paid to his sporting pretensions. It also made it very painful for him to kneel, which, as he was wont to remark ruefully on occasion, was not very helpful in the legitimate pursuit of his chosen profession.

'It's not that God minds, I'm sure,' he once confided to Gauvinier over a pint in the Golden Hind, which was rather more out-of-the-way than the Dog and Duck, 'But the Bishop is most insistent that whoever officiates at the service should be *seen* to be kneeling, particularly while the Nunc Dimittis is being sung.'

'Never mind,' Gauvinier comforted him. 'I'm sure none of

the congregation worries. We've all got our heads down then too.'

'Ah, but people *peep.* Or at least the Bishop says they do.'

Gauvinier decided he'd had enough to eat for the day, poured himself a weak whisky and water and telephoned the vicarage. *So* kind of him to call. Was he too tired after his long day in Town to call over a little later? Or could Mrs Veyzey drive over between the choir practice and the bell-ringing? No, Mr Gauvinier would relish an evening stroll. Could he inquire what was the reason for the call?

'I'd rather not say on the telephone,' said Mrs Veyzey mysteriously. She was one of those persons who were convinced that 'they' listened to every call. Intrigued, Gauvinier changed out of his business clothes by the simple method of removing a black pullover and donning a green one, combed his hair, finished his whisky and, with one stop on the way at the Dog and Duck, strolled over to the vicarage.

Mrs Veyzey was waiting for him.

'You've timed it very nicely,' she said, sitting him down on a faded and brocaded *chaise-longue.* It would have fetched a small fortune in the King's Road. 'We've just got rid of the choirboys and the bell-ringers don't arrive for half an hour, and in any case they won't need their beer until nine o'clock.'

'Beer? Isn't that a little – how shall I say – unclerical?'

'Oh no, it's the traditional drink for the bell-ringers. At one time the incumbent used to brew his own beer especially to keep the ringers going through the night for the long peals. My husband wanted to restore the tradition, but I'm afraid he's not very practical and when he tried to brew his own beer, three bottles exploded all over the pantry. So now we have two jugs sent over from the Dog and Duck every Friday night. I believe they're the same utensils that are used by the cricket club on Saturdays.'

Mrs Veyzey sat solidly upright on her chair, managing to express simultaneous approval of tradition and distaste of beer drinking. It must be difficult for her, Gauvinier thought sympathetically. He made a nondescript noise in his throat.

'What was it you wanted to talk to me about, Mrs Veyzey? Is there anything I can do to help in any way?'

'I don't think it's a question just of help, Mr Gauvinier. It's a question of taking emergency measures. If we don't stop it now, the whole village will be overrun.'

'Stop what, Mrs Veyzey? I don't understand. What is it that you're afraid of? Why don't you start at the beginning and tell me the whole story?'

'Yes, well, I suppose I'd better. But you haven't heard anything about it?'

'Mrs Veyzey, I haven't heard anything about anything.'

She looked at him suspiciously. 'Are you sure? Are you sure you're not just pretending not to know?'

'Mrs Veyzey. How can I possibly know what you're talking about before you've even spoken to me about it? I haven't the faintest idea.'

'Oh. Well then.' Mrs Veyzey collected her breath and began again.

'Did you know that a Very Important Meeting was held this week at Tyling Manor?' She invested the question with capital letters.

'No. All I heard was that James Mitterman and his wife held an expensive dinner party up there on Wednesday.'

'That's it. That's the one.' The vicar's wife drew a deep breath, expanded her bosom, and waded in.

'You are aware that Simpson the butcher has two daughters, Arabella and Araminta?'

Gauvinier nodded.

'Arabella is employed at Tyling Manor as a waitress. She's the pretty one,' she added inconsequentially. 'Sometimes, when they are busy, the banqueting manager, Mr Thompson, gets Araminta to go along in the evening to help. She does it to earn extra money. The tips I am told are excellent. She is saving up to get married.'

'You seem remarkably well informed, Mrs Veyzey.'

''Minta works as a trainee hairdresser at Miss Innes'. Jane's, you know. I went there this morning for my usual trim and set. I don't hold with this permanent waving.' Mrs Veyzey moved her head, as if expecting to admire her hairstyle in an invisible mirror. Gauvinier gave what he hoped was an appreciative nod.

'Well, 'Minta told me that Mr Mitterman and his guests – young Mr Trine was there and Fred Bason the builder, and a very grand man from London with some sort of girl – 'Minta told me that they were talking about some development plans for Tillingfold which could very well affect the cricket ground. So I thought you should be told as soon as possible.'

'Mrs Veyzey, it's flattering of you to suggest that I might be able to do something to stop it. But I can't see they can do anything. The land belongs to the parish council and we're only the sitting tenants, with the soccer club in the winter. It's Scheduled Land, anyway. They can't touch it. It's all part of the Green Belt. I'm sure you're worrying unnecessarily.'

'Well, I do hope you're right. But my husband has been hearing some very distressing rumours recently, and you know he won't do anything about them himself. Richard believes that as man proposes, so the Lord disposes. I hope I do not seem to be letting him down when I say that, sometimes man could do with a little more self help and a little less prayer. He'll be in in a minute. The bell-ringing's just begun.'

As if on cue, the Reverend Richard Veyzey strolled vaguely into the room, greeted Gauvinier with an ecclesiastical gesture of the hand and collapsed into a cavernous chair that appeared to be accustomed to such ill-treatment.

'My dear fellow. My dear fellow. Delighted. Have you had a drink? Oh Sylvia.' He managed to make it sound like the social gaffe of the century, but Mrs Veyzey was unmoved.

'If you'd left enough in the decanter I would have poured Mr Gauvinier a whisky,' she said calmly. 'Now you'll have to find the bottle you've hidden in the toolshed.'

The vicar flushed slightly.

'It's not that I'm an alcoholic,' he said apologetically to Gauvinier. 'But if I hide it, I can never find it, so we can't drink it. And Sylvia is so much stronger-minded than I am. She always knows where it is, but refuses to say so until we have a guest. All right, my dear, I'll get it.' He hurried out, leaving Gauvinier amused but embarrassed.

When he returned, beaming, he poured a full bottle of Johnny Walker into a square cut-glass decanter, which he placed on a tarnished silver tray with two crystal tumblers and a beaker of water. He offered the whole to Gauvinier.

'Help yourself, my dear fellow. Help yourself. No ice, I'm afraid. That blasted machine's broken down again.'

Mr Veyzey purported to regard anything modern as an invention of the devil. The prospect of changing a plug reduced him to despair. His car was a 30-year-old Armstrong Siddeley of the sit-up-and-beg type, maintained in running order at great expense, which he could not afford, by Frank Hunter's garage. He would have preferred a horse and trap, but the Tillingfold parish covered a wide area of the countryside, and some of the roads over the Downs were too steep for four-legged transport. It was a harmless enough affectation, and one which endeared the vicar to Gauvinier, because it meant that the services in Tillingfold Church were still conducted in the Authorized language of King James the First, and the hymns came from the English Hymnal, with all the lovely old vigorous tunes written in minims. The village was divided in its opinions of the vicar. One-third regarded him as a stuck-up old-fashioned anachronism; one-third, like Gauvinier, regarded him with amused affection as the somewhat ridiculous defender of the older values; and the rest forgot that he, or the church, existed at all. Until a father, or mother, or maybe a brother or a cousin, died.

In recent years there had been something of an increase in his Sunday congregations. True, most of the people who attended matins on Sundays were over fifty, but Mr Veyzey had noticed, gradually, that the boys were returning to the choir. In the dark days of the early sixties, on occasion the choir had been reduced to three trebles; old Venables the sidesman had been obliged to sing the alto line in a fluctuating falsetto. But now they were able to sport both decani and cantoris, and the Tillingfold choir began to re-establish the reputation it had held at the turn of the century. It had received help from an unlikely quarter. A few years before, the well-known pop star Albert Jess had quit his group and his chosen profession in a blaze of expensive litigation. He bought Birdwood, an Elizabethan farmhouse just outside Tillingfold with 300 acres of prime farmland attached, and settled down to forget the jet-set and to learn how to farm. For the first year or two he made mistakes, but even after paying a million pounds in compensation to his pop sponsors, there was plenty left to cushion some elementary agricultural errors, and he had the sense to hire local expertise. In a surprisingly short time the farm began to pay its way and Albert Jess, at forty, started to look about him for other fields to occupy his restless intelligence. He was a useful cricketer, and had established himself as a useful opening batsman.

One Sunday morning, quite without volition, he had found himself much to his surprise outside the church as the bells were pealing their merry message. His mind registered automatically that the tenor was flat, but the morning was sunny and the small knots of people in their spring clothes attracted him. Unobtrusively he slipped through the door and sat in one of the rear pews. There was a hint of incense in the air. From his memories, Jess deduced the service would be more Higher than Lower Church, and he was not mistaken. It was the old form of service. The vicar made an imposing figure in his flowing black robe and snow-white cassock; he chanted the Lord's Prayer in a voice which fell a full tone flat. He was obviously tone deaf and Jess was relieved when a curate took over the leading of the responses in a silvery tenor.

'Oh Lord, open Thou our lips,' intoned the priest.

'And our mouth shall shew forth Thy praise,' replied the ready voices of the choir, echoing through the rafters. The congregation supplied a mumbled contrebass.

'Oh God, make speed to save us.'

'Oh Lord, make haste to help us.'

Jess was strangely moved by the nearly forgotten, simple words and rich harmony. He was a born performer, and his spirit lifted to the ancient dramatic formula. The lesson followed, taken from the Book of Kings.

'. . . But I know your sitting down and your going out and coming in, and your raging against me. Because your arrogance has come into my ears I will put my hook in your nose and my bit in your mouth, and I will turn you back on the way by which you came.'

After the service, the vicar hastened to the porch of the church, as he did every Sunday, to shake hands with the congregation and have a sympathetic word with the more elderly of his flock. Jess waited patiently, enjoying the spring sunshine and the bright colour of the daffodils against the grey of the tombstones, until the last farewell had been said and the last hand shaken. Then he introduced himself, diffidently enough. He knew only too well the image the years of maximum publicity had given him. Mr Veyzey seemed quite unaware of his reputation.

'Mr Jess? Ah yes, how pleasant. Welcome to our little church. I see you have come to Birdwood Farm? Such a charming house – I believe the south end is early Elizabethan, is it not? Will you be farming the land? Excellent. Excellent. Dairy farming? Jerseys, you say? Oh, excellent. We were afraid the new owner might be going to introduce those infernal machines. Battery chickens, or the like. I really do believe the mushroom farm is good for the village, so many people work there these days, but for the life of me I cannot believe that a mushroom grown artificially can taste anything like the real thing, now, can it? But then I am accused of being old-fashioned.'

Jess agreed that the natural article was usually better than the plastic product and ventured a mildly congratulatory sentence about the service and the choir.

'I'm so glad you like it. Some people complain that King James's language is dead and incomprehensible to the modern generation, but I am afraid I cannot agree. These modernists are all very well intentioned,' said the vicar, warming to his hobby-horse, 'but I have no doubt that the Church will regret having given way to them in the long run. I am ashamed to confess it, but I cannot attend Billington any more. No choir, guitars in place of the organ. I really don't know what things are coming to.'

Jess found, as many had before him, that it was necessary to check the torrent of the vicar's enthusiasm. He tried to bring the clergyman back to earth with a question about the strength of the choir.

'Oh, yes indeed, we have been so unfortunate. Such a pity though. Our choirmistress, Miss Sims, you know, passed away some months ago. She had been such a loyal friend of the church for more than thirty years, but I must confess she was a little hard of hearing before the end. And young Broadhurst – he's my curate, you know – you heard him lead the responses this morning – has done such a good job for us since Miss Sims died. But now he is leaving to accept a living in Yorkshire. We are all so pleased for him, but it will leave our choir headless, as it were. Mr Brown, the bass, will no doubt try, but he hasn't the training, you know, and the boys will not pay attention to him. Do you know, last week when Mr Broadhurst was away for his interview, Mr Brown took the choir practice in the vicarage dining-room, and after it Mrs Veyzey found parallel scratches all down the refectory table. She was most upset. Apparently young Jimmy Slocombe and Dickie Hunter had been sliding the cat on the polished surface – they pretended the poor creature was a racing car – and it used its claws to try to stop. Like brakes, you know. Mrs Veyzey was *most* put out. I'm afraid that's the end of choir practice in the dining-room. They'll have to go back to the Lady chapel, but it's very difficult when the bell-ringers want to begin early, and Friday's the only day they can all manage to come.'

Jess managed to dam the flow by offering to coach the choir until a suitable replacement could be found for the departing

Mr Broadhurst. And the vicar, delighted that anyone should come forward but also convinced that He had in fact moved in His mysterious ways yet again, gratefully accepted. He did not even ask Jess whether he was qualified.

Twenty-eight years previously Albert Jess's voice had broken and he was ejected from the choir of St Martin's, Billington with a sigh of relief from the rector, whose life he had made a misery. Most of the intervening years had been spent with a guitar in his hands and a microphone at his mouth. Yet he was a competent musician, and he soon discovered that the pop tune and the hymn are not so far apart after all. He read music well, and was equally at home on the keyboard as on the strings. At first he used the ancient upright piano in the vestry for choir practice, but someone unearthed an old harmonium from a storeroom, surprisingly free of woodworm, and he dusted it down and found it in working order.

To one who had handled the vagaries and temperamental quirks of the popular music industry for the biggest part of his working life, establishing discipline among the younger and more lively choristers was easy. He had two degrees of punishment. The offender was given the choice of leaving the choir altogether or standing on his head in the corner of the room. There was no mid-way point. During his second practice, the vicar, looking in to see if everything was going well for his new choirmaster, saw three young gentlemen head-standing, their feet against the wall. He was surprised, and a little concerned.

'Isn't it harmful?' he asked Jess anxiously.

'Not a bit of it. It's a well-known yoga position. Clears the brain of evil thoughts. It works, you know, Vicar,' he explained cheerfully. 'They sing much better afterwards, don't you Slocombe?' He addressed the afterthought to the middle of the upside-down boys, who said, 'Yes, Bert,' in a strangulated voice.

'Don't worry, he's fine. They get used to it after five minutes or so.'

The vicar shook his head and withdrew. He knew better than to interfere, and his wisdom paid off as recruits to the choir came flooding in and Jess was able to hold auditions to weed out the tone-deaf and totally impossible.

'I don't give a damn what you sing, so long as you all sing the same thing and you begin and end it together.' Adapting Sir Thomas Beecham's dictum, he stuck to simple things, getting intonation, diction and clarity of tone right before he tried anything more elaborate. He bought records of church music performed by choirs like that of King's College, Cambridge, and studied them at home before trying out a new hymn. At Christmas time, greatly daring, he produced a Festival of Carols, enlisting the students at the Billington Music Centre to accompany the choir; the vicar conducted the service, reading every other lesson with a firm vibrant voice, and beaming at the biggest congregation the church had witnessed in forty years. Among those attending was a young reporter from the county *Times* in Billington, doing the stint as part of his paper's annual 'Christmas round-up'.

'Go to church, you young sod,' said his news editor. 'It'll do you good. We only want a couple of paras to tuck in the round-up, and you live over there. It'll save travelling exes.'

'But not overtime.' Phillip Renton was a keen union man. He was also a good reporter, and he turned in his two paragraphs written in the style of his newspaper.

'Carol Service at Tillingfold,' ran the headline. 'Tillingfold Anglican church was pleasingly filled for the festival of Nine Carols and Nine Lessons. The Reverend Arthur Veyzey, Vicar of Tillingfold, read the lessons, together with leading local citizens, and the excellent choir was conducted by Mr Albert Jess of Birdwood Farm.'

The county *Times* was due to be published on Friday. On Thursday afternoon, Renton, who besides being a keen union man had an eye for the main chance, dialled a well-known Fleet Street number and spoke to the deputy news editor.

'. . . all right. I'll put the copy over. And I'll send the negative on the three-thirty train from Billington, Red Star. Thank you, Mr Preston. Thank you.'

And the next day the *Daily Bugle*, grateful for anything out of the ordinary on a dull news day, carried a slightly fuzzy picture of Albert Jess, resplendent in cassock and surplice, conducting; under his raised right arm was vaguely visible the decani row of choristers and over the top was the headline: 'Pop Star Gets in the Groove with God.'

All of this took the vicar quite a considerable time to recount, and Gauvinier, who had heard much of it before, had finished his first large whisky and water and was well embarked on his second and was beginning to wonder when his host would come to the point.

'Arthur,' Mrs Veyzey was gentle but firm. 'I was talking to Mr Gauvinier about the rumours about what is going to happen to the cricket club. That's what he's come over for tonight. Why don't you tell him what happened at the parish council meeting?'

'Oh, very well, my dear.' Mr Veyzey was not in the slightest put out. He was used to direction in matters other than those which concerned the Church.

'I can't really tell you very much, Peter. I wasn't listening too carefully. But I gathered from what the chairman said that we can expect to get before the next meeting a letter from the county planning people. Apparently they've got wind of a scheme some businessmen have put forward to build on the cricket pitch – a depot or something – and they want to know if we'll have any objection. Nobody knows anything more about it until we get the letter; so we've no idea whether it is to be a serious proposition or not. I'm afraid I just laughed. I can't see the village agreeing to let the ground go. After all, it's the recreation ground as well, and the war memorial's there. They can't be serious . . . at least I didn't think so until I heard about the dinner at Tyling Manor the other night.'

'What's that got to do with it?'

'I don't know, Peter. But I do know that your friend Mitterman was entertaining Sir Philip Beeston at Tyling Manor this week. Lomax, the manager there, told me. There was nothing secret about it, although he said they seemed to take some pains not to be conspicuous – tucked away at a corner table. And Fred Bason was there too, and young Trine.'

'It's an unlikely combination for dinner, I know,' said Gauvinier. 'But what's so suspicious about it?'

An expression almost intelligent flickered across the unworldly face of the Reverend Mr Veyzey.

'Oh, didn't you know? Beeston's the head of Superstores. I went to college with him. At the risk of sounding un-Christian, I must say he is one of the most unpleasant men it's ever been my misfortune to meet.'

Chapter 4

The selection committee of Tillingfold Cricket Club met every Tuesday evening during the season to choose the teams for the following weekend : one for Saturday, sometimes two for Sunday and occasionally there was a Colts' XI to select as well, or a team for one of these new-fangled six-a-side competitions which seemed to be catching on. The four men met, if it was fine, in the pavilion after the Tuesday evening practice or, if it was wet, occasionally they might gather in Gauvinier's cottage. It was a routine that had been established for six years now, ever since Gauvinier had been first elected skipper of the team and, *ex officio*, chairman of the selection committee.

Even with so many teams to pick, the meeting rarely lasted longer than an hour. With twenty-three adult (over eighteen) playing members and a variable figure of about ten Colts, there was not a wide choice. And yet the weekly selection committee meeting weighed heavily on Gauvinier's mind the moment the previous weekend's games were finished. He found that this apparently simple task of choosing eleven fit and able men to represent the village of Tillingfold demanded patience and tact, and a psychological expertise which would have tried the wisdom of Solomon.

Non-cricketers and foreigners (Gauvinier and other enthusiasts were inclined to lump them all together) failed to understand or appreciate the importance in their lives of this patently absurd game which they loved so much. Cricket had cost Gauvinier one marriage, and his second survived only through the loving tolerance of the quite exceptional woman who was Polly. Gauvinier had never heard of anyone who had actually killed for cricket's sake (a plus mark he usually dredged up as the discussion thickened with the smoke around closing time), but he knew several who had cheated and lied for it; just as there were men like the vice-president of a village club close by Tillingfold who made a standing offer of a prize of £5 to any home batsman who could break a window in his house, which stood conveniently just over the boundary at long-off. On a higher plane, there are people who will cheerfully pay a premium of £5,000 for a view overlooking the county ground at Hove; and Gauvinier knew one man who had waited more than twelve years to purchase a flat in the house Sussex had once built for Ranjitsinhji. In Gauvinier's case he loved cricket as some men loved art, or music, continually finding new delight in a game in which every move was an infinitely subtle variation on what had occurred so many times before.

'Of course I know it's only a game.' Gauvinier would laugh shamefacedly to himself when trapped in some hyperbole. And yet at the same time he knew how his namesake Peter felt when he denied his Christ, and waited for the cock to crow. He knew too that each and every member of the team he would lead out on Saturday would share this incomprehensible feeling in some degree. What motives each had for playing, Gauvinier could sometimes divine. How each man felt as the game progressed, what went on in his mind as a wicket tumbled or a catch flew wide of an outstretched hand, he could only guess at. Gauvinier, normally a reasonably sensitive individual, felt his every nerve-end alive during a cricket match, reaching out and all but physically touching every man in the side, drawing him in and willing him to share this almost mystic sense of co-existence. Only before a dry and inflexible personality like that of James Mitterman, secretary-treasurer, did Gauvinier's spirit quail; and yet he was fully aware that the club needed Mitterman's expertise and financial acumen as much as, if not more than, it needed his own drive and enthusiasm and cricket instinct.

On the day in question, the committee took somewhat longer over their deliberations. The match under discussion was rather more important than usual – more so even than the annual Raveley fixture. It was the prestige match of the year. Sunday, 17 July, was President's Day. And this year, the President, Colonel Sir Edgar Trine, DSO, KCMG, had promised to bring the strongest team ever to be seen in Tillingfold. There would be marquees, side-shows, and a bar; and the proceeds would go to charity. The President himself would stand both teams lunch and tea in the village hall and there would be free beer for both teams.

Gauvinier had taken the trouble to write down the names of each of the twenty-three members and of the eight paid-up Colts. Against each name he had entered their state of availability, obtained during the past few days, and a brief note of his own assessment. He kept the list in his pocket, but he never attended a selection meeting unprepared. It was one of the reasons why he was regarded as a good captain. There was always a great deal more than mere cricketing merit to be considered in any Tillingfold team selection.

The committee settled itself round the bare trestle table. Someone had switched on the single light bulb overhead, for although there was plenty of westering light outside, the wooden shutters were still up outside the windows, and the interior of the pavilion was cool and gloomy. Oliver Fanshawe sat gravely, as he always did, his back ramrod straight but inclined slightly forward so that his folded arms rested on the table. As the club umpire he was a member of the selection committee on the grounds of his impartiality, his long experience and close observation of form from behind the stumps. Fred Bason, back from the table, spread his bulk massively on his chair. From behind, his haunches bulged on both sides. His great red hands plumped down on his thighs. Beside him Bill Budgeon shuffled his behind awkwardly on the chair. He had only been elected to the committee this year, and he was not yet accustomed to the unaccustomed responsibility. As a near cripple, with his left leg permanently damaged from a childhood attack of polio, he struggled to make a living as the village's last remaining shoe repairer, and for most of his thirty-five years had regarded himself, and had been regarded by all but a few, as pretty well trodden upon by the rest of the world. Only those in the cricket club could appreciate the depths of courage and determination that had enabled him to become a bowler respected and, on his day, feared for miles around.

Gauvinier ran quickly through the names of those players not available. 'Deacon, he's away on holiday. That's a damned nuisance, but young Trine doesn't mind standing in as wicket-keeper. There's a new man who's just come to the village, Jones, or Jonas I think his name is, wants to join and says he has kept wicket in the past, but I don't want to play him in the President's game first thing off without having a look at him. Anyway, we haven't a clue what his standard may be.

'Cotterell and Furze-Green are both away, and Frank Hunter says he might not be available, which leaves a bit of a shortage of bowlers. That's nothing new. But Simpson also said he might be called away by his firm and that will leave a big hole in the batting.

'Let's start, if we may, with the certainties.'

There were nods and a general mumbling of assent.

'What's Frank playing, hard to get?' Fanshawe had little time for Hunter, whose mercurial personality made what he considered to be unnecessary difficulties for the club, both on and off the field.

Gauvinier grinned. 'Oh, the usual, I suppose. But I do know he's short-handed. He's even taken on young Bobby for the summer holidays and he can't be much use yet.'

He dismissed Hunter with a shrug. He knew his man. When

it came down to it Frank Hunter would play, and be glad to be playing. But there was no doubt that life would be quite a bit easier without Hunter's sudden tergiversations.

'Right, gentlemen, let's go through the order first, and fill in the gaps afterwards. Remember, we want our strongest team out this weekend. Sir Edgar means to "do" us after last year.'

He fished a notebook from his pocket, opened it and wrote 'July 17: President's Game' at the top of a new page.

'Openers. Jess for number one. Agreed?'

They murmured assent. Jess preferred playing lower down, but he had established himself as a useful opening batsman since joining the club a couple of seasons ago. The ex-pop singer had proved a distinct asset to the club and to the village, which had rapidly grown accustomed to his lilac Corniche and flamboyant visitors from London.

'Number two.' Gauvinier hesitated slightly. 'I know James has been occupying the position for the past two seasons, but we really do want to turn out our strongest side. What d'you think?'

There was an embarrassed silence. Fanshawe coughed. He was never one to baulk at an awkward situation. But he gave his friend the opportunity to bring the issue out into the open himself.

'I don't think that's quite all the story, Peter,' he suggested gently.

'Well, no.' Gauvinier was grateful to be made to face the issue squarely. 'I'm in a difficult position here, and you all know it. Personalities mustn't come into it, but there's no denying that I don't see eye to eye with James Mitterman. I'm trying to ignore that and, looking at the fact that we want our strongest team out, he shouldn't be chosen. His top score in two years has been eighteen, and he was dropped twice then. And there's nowhere in an important match that I can hide a bad fielder. Frankly, he's frightened of the hard ball.'

He spoke directly to Fanshawe.

'And I'm *not* thinking about last Sunday. I'd have done that to anyone. And have.'

'Right enough, Peter. But it wasn't very tactful. And honestly

I don't think it'll be in the interests of the club to drop him from the side for the President's game.'

Fred Bason grunted.

'Seems to me it depends whether you run this club by politics or common sense. The man's a damn good secretary we can't afford to lose. As a cricketer he's a dead loss but he doesn't know it, or won't admit it. It's heads you win, tails I lose.'

Bason had a way of saying out loud what other people were thinking. Gauvinier wished with all his heart that you could run a village team on sheer cricketing merit, and yet he was well aware that things didn't work out like that.

The affairs of the cricket club, like those of the Women's Institute, the Conservative Club, the soccer club and a dozen more institutions, were inextricably bound up with personalities and the rest of the village. Whatever was decided here tonight would have some effect somewhere. It sometimes seemed to him as though, being part of the lifeblood of the village, anything they did would affect, for better or worse, the whole tenor of life and indeed, in extreme cases, the course of the village's history. Gauvinier knew it was absurd that, without one of the four actually saying anything to anyone, the course of the discussion, the individual opinions of each member, the division of the vote, if any, would be public property within half an hour of the team's being posted on the village notice board. It was one of the few things about village life that he feared, while accepting it as inevitable. His knowledge did not stop him kicking a little against it.

'What do you think, Bill?' He appealed to Budgeon, who'd been sitting with his hands clasped between his knees, looking at the floor. The shoemaker rubbed his left knee, the bad one, subconsciously. It was a familiar gesture.

'Well, boss, 'ten't really for me to say. But I reckon Mr Mitterman's earned his place. He's played reg'lar, and 'e's paid reg'lar, and 'e's done a bloody good job with club books. 'Ten't only cricket as counts.'

Gauvinier looked at them. It was time to make a decision.

'Well, gentlemen, it looks as if we split two–two, if we were to take a vote, which we won't. That would give me a casting vote, as chairman of the committee.'

He paused, and they looked at him expectantly. Not for the first time in his life, Gauvinier wished his head would not interfere with the convictions of his heart. Then: 'That being so, and it being the chairman's duty to maintain the *status quo*, I vote Mitterman in at number two.' Strangely, the old formula helped.

He wrote down the name on his piece of paper. Someone sighed, audibly. Gauvinier suspected it was himself.

'Number three. Fred, as usual?'

Fred Bason turned slightly red, took a deep breath, and then leaned forward earnestly.

'Look, Peter, I don't mind standing down for this one—' He held up his hand to still a chorus of protest. '—no, I mean it. I'm not as young as I used to be, and I'm not so slippy in the field. I know you want your best team out and it's time some of us old 'uns gave the youngsters a chance.'

Gauvinier looked at his broad face and serious blue eyes. He knew why the offer had been made, and he knew too that Bason was desperately longing for it to be turned down. He grinned.

'I wouldn't hear of it, Fred. You're six years younger than I am, and I've never seen you back away from a ball yet. Number three it is. We want fifty from you this week.'

He wrote the name on his list.

'Can we skip four and five for a moment? I'll put myself in at number six. Leave out seven and eight for a bit, too, and for nine, ten, eleven read Trine, Smith and Budgeon. OK everyone?'

'Nine's a bit low for young Trine, Peter?' Bason made the statement sound like a query.

'Not really, for this match. To my mind he's only in the side at all because Joe Deacon's away. I reckon he'll enjoy being able to let himself go being down the order. With any luck the bowlers will be tired.'

Smith and Budgeon were the stock bowlers, fast and slow-medium respectively. Gauvinier himself bowled slow left-arm as first or second change; Bason could turn an arm over with slow off-breaks, and Hunter bowled fast erratic leg-breaks with a whirlwind action. It was not enough, or good enough, Gauvinier knew, to oppose a side which would contain four or five batsmen at or near county class. Most villages around seemed to be able to find one or two 'stock' bowlers of the old type – six paces run up, steady on a length, and turn your arm over all day. Not Tillingfold. Young and quick, old and true, was the local village saying, and so it had been for years. They eventually settled on Hunter number eight. 'That'll please him, I don't think,' Budgeon muttered to himself while Fred Bason merely grinned. At number seven they placed a schoolboy named Haynes, who not only bowled left-arm fast, but was also a promising batsman and an enthusiastic fieldsman in the deep.

That left the batsmen at number four and five to be chosen and, as Gauvinier said, there was an embarrassment not so much of riches as of mediocrity. After some heart-searching they preferred Paul White at number four to the Reverend Arthur Veyzey, who came in at number five because, said Bason, 'He can always pray for rain and for White's soul.' Paul White was a brilliant natural cricketer who Gauvinier believed could have scaled the highest peaks, but who seemed intent on wasting away his many talents in protest and pop music. The village had been 'giving him time' since he was twelve years old, and only such perpetual optimists as Gauvinier persisted in their hope to see young White in prosperous progressive employment. At twenty, he spent his summers as a lifeguard at various resorts on the South coast, and his winters reading electricity meters. He had already sired two babies that he knew of, and it was part of his undoubted attraction that each of five girls in different parts of the county believed that he was exclusively engaged to her. He drank spirits insatiably, apparently with little adverse effect on his abilities or equilibrium, and smoked forty cigarettes a day. Gauvinier, who had no children of his own, regarded him as the acme of all that was wrong with the youth of today, yet couldn't help liking him and wishing he'd had half the youngster's natural ability. The

Rev. Mr Veyzey (Gauvinier deplored to the depths of his being the current idiom of referring to 'Reverend Veyzey', a habit spread by the BBC from its innumerable news items on 'Reverend Paisley' of Northern Ireland and 'Reverend Sithole' of Rhodesia), the vicar was a large untidy batsman in his middle forties, who was liable to produce an exquisite late cut in the midst of an innings of unbelievable banality, but who indeed had made many useful, if lucky, scores for Tillingfold. As he said, his congregation could increase by as much as fifty per cent (or thirty people) the day after he scored a quick half-century. He conceded that mercifully it didn't drop correspondingly each time he made a duck. With his floppy grey hair and his craggy lined face, Mr Veyzey made an impressive member of the Tillingfold team, the more so because he wore a quartered cap whose colours had long since faded to a uniform grey. 'Harlequins,' the cognoscenti would mutter behind the back of their hands, and nod sagely to each other, and Gauvinier would laugh to himself and wink at the vicar, who had won a scholarship to Jesus, Cambridge, from Salcombe Grammar School.

This, then, was the team that Gauvinier posted on the pavilion door that night, on the village noticeboard half an hour later, and which he dropped in the next morning to the county *Times* office on his way to London.

Tillingfold CC v. President's XI
Sunday, 17th July,
Start at 11.30 a.m.

1. A. Jess
2. J. B. Mitterman
3. F. Bason
4. P. White
5. Rev. A. Veyzey
6. P. Gauvinier (Capt.)
7. A. Haynes
8. F. Hunter
9. R. E. Trine

10. N. Smith
11. B. Budgeon
Umpire: Mr. O. B. Fanshawe.

It was the custom of the selection committee to adjourn after its weekly meeting to the Dog and Duck and to slake the thirst brought on by an hour or so of hard talking and thinking with a pint or two of the real ale George Buller kept back for his regular customers. As they walked slowly across from the Post Office Stores, where Gauvinier had pinned up his team notice (he had a key to the glass-fronted noticeboard), he broached the subject that had been nagging at him since his visit to the vicarage.

'Fred, what's all this development being planned that's going to affect the cricket ground?'

The builder didn't look at Gauvinier. He stared straight ahead of him at the pavement, keeping his eyes down as if he was intent, like Pooh, on not tripping over the joins between the paving stones. Eventually he spoke.

'Well,' he began slowly, 'I reckon it's all pie in the sky at the moment, but if it comes off it'll do mighty well for the village. Sort of bring it up to date, if you see what I mean.'

'Not really, Fred, until you tell us what it's all about.'

'Oh, you won't like it, Mr Gauvinier.'

Gauvinier stared at him. It was fifteen years since Fred Bason, who could have bought Gauvinier without taking his hand from his trouser pocket, had used the formal style of address.

'Why? What's it to do with me?'

Bason sighed. His Sussex burr broadened.

''Ten't nothin' to do with 'ee, surr. But it'll mean the end of the cricket club – or at least the end of cricket on the cricket field. That Beeston plans to build a complex of supermarkets clean across it. 'Twon't only be the cricket field of course. Mr Jess's land at Birdwood which is adjoining will mostly go, too. The whole scheme is going to cost more than twenty millions.'

Gauvinier stared at him. It was difficult to comprehend.

'Twenty millions? You must be joking. No one's going to spend twenty millions on Tillingfold! And what d'you mean, the cricket field? No one can have that. It belongs to the council and it's part of the Green Belt. The village was promised that your estate would be the last development allowed in Tillingfold. You remember the row over that, Fred, of all people.'

They entered the pub at that moment. Bason waited until Gauvinier, as was customary, bought the first round of half-pints (it used to be pints until inflation sent the beer up to 40p a go) and they settled round one of the bare tables in the skittles parlour.

'It's the new development principle. The multiple stores don't want exclusive sites any more. They like to be all together so that they can attract each other's customers. Have you seen the Brent Cross scheme?'

They shook their heads. There was little cause for natives of Tillingfold to trudge over to the north-west of London for their shopping.

'It's a complex of major stores with acres of free parking. Even the big Oxford Street stores are there, and Harrods. The idea is that you can do all your West End shopping without having to traipse up to the West End. The Beeston scheme is for the same sort of thing for the south-east, but drawing its customers from everywhere from Dover to Southampton and Reading. They reckon Tillingfold is just the right position. The potential market's as big as Greater London itself, if you include Croydon and all the Surrey towns.'

'But the big firms like Marks and Spencer won't stand for it. Surely it'll take customers away from all the supermarkets they've built in Brighton and Crawley, and Raveley and Horsham and everywhere else. It'll never pay.'

'Don't you believe it. They'll go along with it. Once Beeston's got one of the groups, the others daren't be left out. Like the Brighton Marina. Once the thing's started it just rolls along like a juggernaut.'

Fanshawe brought the discussion down to the particular.

'Just what will you make out of this, Fred? Are you going to build the thing? I should have thought it was a bit out of your line.'

'Oh, no, not me. It's far too big for a little local builder. They've asked me to go on the board, as a local industrialist, and I'll get as much, if not more, of the sub-contracts than I can handle. I shouldn't have to work again for the rest of my life.'

'And Mitterman? Where does he come in?'

'Oh, James.' Bason's voice was disenchanted. 'James Mitterman's the bloke in the middle. He's fixed it all up for Beeston. He'll come off best of all – I reckon at fifteen per cent he'll make nearer five million than four out of this little lot.'

He grinned a little defensively.

'I know people will say we're ruining the village. I said so myself at first. But I must admit that the prospect of making fifty thousand or so out of it is better than nothing as compensation, and if it's going to go ahead anyway there's no point in not getting in on the act.'

Gauvinier found his voice.

'What d'you mean, going ahead anyway? Surely any scheme like this can be killed at birth. The parish can wreck it by refusing to sell the land. This is supposed to be Green Belt.'

'Oh, Mitterman's told Beeston that he's got all that side of it fixed. I know if you get the Department on your side even what the county says means nothing at all. The parish council doesn't stand an earthly. And James hinted that they might well be on his side anyway.'

Fanshawe had been growing quieter and more pensive. Now he looked up.

'Just how far has this thing gone, Fred?'

'I don't know, Mr Fanshawe. Probably not as far as they – er, we – would like. But there'll have to be a public inquiry when any objections will be heard.'

'Oh, yes, Fred. I think you can take it there'll be objections.'

They broke up quietly, each with his own thoughts. Budgeon, who had taken no part in the conversation, cycled home, confused and angry. Once again the very foundations of his life seemed to be threatened. He had few illusions that there would be room in the Tillingfold of the future for 'Budgeon – Shoemaker' whether the new complex was to be built or not. The best he could hope for, he knew, was to carry on repairing the stylish Italian leather shoes of Teddy Trine and his friends, or making the occasional shoe for one of the better-off landowners thereabouts. Even in the late nineteen seventies, he reflected, there were people whom he'd known as a child as 'the gentry' who could still afford the affectation of referring to 'my shoemaker'. It was a better weapon in the battle of one-upmanship than 'my dressmaker', or 'my hairdresser' or 'my tailor', possibly ranking with 'my trainer' or 'my saddler' among the horsy set and falling short only of something like 'my yachtbuilder'. Even Budgeon these days had 'my accountant' – and indeed, he thought ruefully, 'my accountant' was that same James Mitterman. He wondered what Mitterman could be doing dealing with his own simple affairs for a pittance, when there were millions to be made by destroying a village and a way of life at the lift of a finger. In which he was doing an injustice to Mitterman, for the accountant had undertaken to deal with 'Budgeon – Shoemaker's' VAT business out of kindness and sympathy, and without the very tiniest of notions deep down that this was insurance against some as yet unforeseen evil that might affect the smooth running of the Mitterman masterplan. If he had thought of it at all, Mitterman in any case might have reckoned the saving of Bill Budgeon from the VATman as very small beer to balance the mountain of plot and counter-plot which signified his successful passage through life so far. Mitterman believed in no god, but he did believe that he who had no insurance against the unexpected was a fool. And he did not intend to be taken as a fool, even after death.

Bason climbed into his scarlet Montefiori and drove home slowly to the foursquare modern villa on the outskirts of the village. He had built it with a small part of the profit he'd made on four Elizabethan cottages he'd bought in the fifties for £250 each and sold in the seventies, tastefully renovated, for £20,000 apiece. Fred Bason was no sentimentalist, and he felt little remorse at the prospect of making a great deal of money from the scheme he had outlined to the others. There was a fleeting regret, perhaps, at the end of cricket on the field it had occupied for more than 150 years, but Bason promised himself that he'd 'see the cricket club all right'. He resolved that his first objective would be to find another field and pay for a new pavilion.

On the way to his bachelor home he passed Hunter's Garage, with the Hunter household attached. Every room in house and garage shone bright with electric lights, and Fred shook his head to himself, reflecting that the amount of electricity Frank wasted each year would pay for the new timing gear he'd been moaning he couldn't afford for the business. The kitchen window, like the rest of the building, was brightly lit and the curtains were open. He glimpsed Frank, red-faced like himself, leaning on the kitchen table and saying something angrily to Rosie. She was standing arms akimbo on the other side of the table and glaring at Frank. The Fiat swept on, leaving the cameo in Fred Bason's mind of a scene to be part of which, for all its impression of anger, he would have cheerfully given up every penny of the profit he hoped to make on the Tillingfold Complex. For once Fred Bason had wooed and so nearly won Rosie Verrall, only to see his best friend and one-time partner, Frank Hunter, snatch her away, a week from the altar.

Gauvinier and Fanshawe walked home together in silence. Their ways lay along the same route, for Fanshawe's house and garden abutted on Gauvinier's older cottage. Fanshawe's home was an anachronism, a red-brick Victorian elaboration standing plush and foursquare amid small cottages, whitewashed lath and plaster and stucco, out of character and out of countenance with its surroundings. Even its garden, walled on three sides in pebble and brick, bore little relation to any building within miles. Fanshawe, delving among the records, had unearthed the history, and had renamed it 'The Railway House' to explain the whole thing in his usual rational, logical fashion. There was no railway station, or indeed a railway line, nearer than seven miles away at Billington. But in the heyday of railway construction, in the eighteen fifties, when Brunel and his cronies were buying up land clean across the country and laying thousands of miles of 'permanent way', just one such scheme was expected to embrace Tillingfold. But the revered nineteenth-century planners made mistakes just as their heirs and successors were to do in the twentieth century, and someone built a 'railway house' long before the railway was due to come to Tillingfold. 'But they built to last in those days,' Fanshawe told Gauvinier and indeed the two-up, two-down foursquare little house exactly matched the unfashionable character of its owner, who could be just as pawky and obstinate and upright as any nineteenth-century stationmaster.

They did not talk much on the walk home, each busy with his own thoughts. But when they arrived Fanshawe shooed Gauvinier through the white-painted wicker gate and up the neat brick path. He let them both in, and as he busied himself finding a whisky-and-soda for them both, Gauvinier settled in one of the crinkled leather armchairs, adjusted himself to the hint of sag in the upholstery and wondered for the umpteenth time at the efficiency of the bachelor male. He had once spent two weeks in a Lagos hotel sharing a room with an unmarried reporter (at a time of gross overcrowding during the Biafran war) and had been shamed then by the neat rows of suits, each on its own hanger, which emerged from the immaculate travelling bag. Fawcett, he recalled, always had spare razor blades, toothpaste, malaria tablets, and Alka-Seltzer, while from his own suitcase tumbled a crumpled assorted mixture of shirts and slacks and underpants, his one good outfit ruined by the aerosol after-shave which had de-pressurized in mid-flight. He had come to the conclusion that the contrast was caused by the simple fact that Fawcett had always fended for himself, and had developed a fail-safe, foolproof self-sufficiency that the pampered Gauvinier, who had been married to one woman or another for longer than he cared to recall, would never reach.

Fanshawe's character was reflected in the brown severity of the room's furnishings, the small but comprehensive library of classical literature embalmed in its glass-fronted bookcase, the wide desk with its pigeonholes packed in orderly fashion and a pile of reference books stacked awaiting Fanshawe's next project. An upright Steinway stood along one wall away from the fireplace, for after his recovery from injury Fanshawe had learnt to play and, although he would never be expert, had attained a standard whereby he could occupy himself for hours wrestling with the intricacies of Chopin, the subtleties of Schumann and the grandeur of Beethoven. In two series of shelves, stretching both sides of the dark oak fireplace, were arrayed every volume of Wisden, from the priceless number one, and including virtually unobtainable volumes from World War I years, to number 114. And with them, a selection of cricket books which must have been rivalled only by the library at Lord's, from the poems of the great John Nyren to the polished clichés of Arlott. From the wall, a caricature by Spy of Fanshawe's grandfather, who had played for Surrey against the great W. G. Grace. Robert Fanshawe, QC, gazed severely down, the image of his grandson with his face set in absurdly straight lines, from the square cheekbones to the vertical furrows running from the sides of the nose nearly to the chin, and the parallels of pain etched into the forehead above the little fans of humour round the unexpectedly gentle eyes.

Fanshawe was frowning as he handed Gauvinier his whisky.

'Just what are we going to do, Peter? Is there any stopping something like this? How far can they have got? And, of course, will the village want it stopped?' They both knew that one of the many divisions in Tillingfold's corporate existence was that between the so-called progressives and the traditionalists. But Gauvinier had been thinking hard during the stroll back from the meeting. Although he had quite deliberately forgotten any military training he might have absorbed, his experience of advertising campaigns had taught him the need for thorough preparation, assessment of the opposition and analysis of his own position. His captain's mind was in business again.

'Look,' he said thoughtfully. 'The position's this. Beeston and Mitterman have this big scheme for making money, and for some reason or other they've decided they can do it in Tillingfold. They've obviously been planning it for months. But equally obviously they haven't got far enough ahead with it yet to let the scheme get out into the open. Hence the secrecy. When they're ready to release it it will be splurged about as an accomplished fact that no one can stop. They've probably gone quite a long way towards it, but they're not there yet. They've obviously had to tread very carefully after all the land and development scandals of the past ten years. Right, so that's weakness number one in their plan. They're frightened of too much early publicity.

'Weakness number two is that although they have a good idea who the opposition is bound to be, they don't know how strong or widespread any campaign is likely to be. Correspondingly, we don't know how quickly we can mount anything effective, or even if we can do it in time.

'And weakness number three is hypothetical, but it assumes that they must be sailing pretty near the wind or are prepared to be downright illegal, to force this thing through. We've got to try to catch them out.

'My first thought is the parish council. Then the rural district, and then the county council, in that order. If we don't have any luck with that lot, then it looks like the Minister of the Environment and a public inquiry, just like the motorway inquiries and Windscale, with organized protests, the lot.

'My second thought is Phillip Renton. And my third is the cricket club.'

Fanshawe, who had nodded his head through most of this discourse, looked up sharply.

'The cricket club? I know it's affected, but I don't see there's much it can do other than to add its voice to the general protest.'

'Someone's got to lead that protest. Why not the cricket club? If the parish council won't, or can't, provide the opposition, then we'll have to fight for ourselves.'

Gauvinier took a swig at his whisky and warmed to his theme.

'I know you love cricket, Oliver, but would you actually fight for it?'

Fanshawe reflected carefully.

'Stupidly enough, probably before a number of things other people might consider much more important.'

'That's right. And it's my belief that a hell of a lot more people exist like us. Any cause needs a focal point, and the cricket club can provide it. Nobody's going to go to the stocks for Tillingfold's beauty, or its history. We just haven't got enough of either for it to be important. But if, just for once, a cricket club set up a cry for help, I think we'd all be surprised at what might happen.

'It isn't just politics, it's deeper than that. I'm no Tory. In fact if I'm scratched I'm probably just another wishy-washy liberal under the skin without enough guts or ideals to prevent either of the major parties doing their worst with this country. But I'm damned if I'll let some fart-arse with a bulldozer plough up our cricket pitch.'

Gauvinier paused, embarrassed at his own anger and surprised at his own vehemence. It took a great deal to make him swear.

'What happens if they offer you another cricket pitch?' asked Fanshawe mildly.

'That's beside the point. Cricket has been played on Tillingfold's ground for 140 years at the least, to the best of our knowledge. It probably goes back another couple of hundred years before that. My father planted one of those chestnut trees and I'm not going to be the one to chop it down – or let anyone else loose with a damned great axe. Sling me the directory.'

He deftly caught the bulky telephone directory and thumbed through it swiftly. He was lucky to run his quarry to earth in the second pub he rang.

'Mr. Renton? Sorry to disturb you at this time of night. You don't know me. My name's Gauvinier, captain of the Tillingfold Cricket Club. Is it possible for you to pop over and see me tonight? I've got a story for you, and it's exclusive. Or I can drive over to Billington if you prefer . . . You'll come over? That's good of you. What do you drink? Whisky – it'll be waiting. The address is . . . oh, you know it? Good. See you in half an hour.'

He cradled the phone gently, smiling at his friend.

'Now tell me I'm an impetuous idiot who's about to do more harm than good.'

'You're an impetuous idiot who's about to do more harm than good. What can I do to help you commit mayhem?'

'Come round to my place and drink my whisky for a change, and see what we can cook up between us before Renton gets here. I've an idea that young man's going to get a lot more than he's bargained for.'

Chapter 5

In the forty-five minutes before the journalist arrived, Gauvinier and Fanshawe had accomplished a great deal more than thought. They had established a de facto Save Tillingfold Action Committee with Gauvinier in the chair and Fanshawe, Jess and the vicar as members. Polly Gauvinier, dragged none too reluctantly from her television set, volunteered to make coffee and sandwiches and act as secretary. The Reverend Richard Veyzey and Albert Jess were telephoned and, enjoying the conspiracy, were round at Gauvinier's cottage within ten minutes and taking a lively part in the discussions.

Renton pulled up on the gravel drive with a squeal of brakes and a rattle from the exhaust pipe. It was a warm night, and Gauvinier had left the front door open and the hall light on. Renton breezed through it without knocking and straight into the big living-room where they were talking.

'Hullo, there,' he cried. 'I'm Renton. Thanks for calling. What can I do you for?' He laughed heartily. He was a brash young man. But he faltered slightly as he focused and identified Jess and the vicar.

'Mr Veyzey. Mr Jess,' he began hesitantly.

'Don't worry, Renton,' said Jess easily. 'It's not one of my nights for kicking journalists.' He referred to the never-to-be-forgotten evening when he floored one of Fleet Street's senior gossip columnists. It had been worth every one of the ten thousand pounds it had cost him, he said.

'Good. I'm glad about that,' said Renton uneasily, and addressed himself to Gauvinier.

'You're Mr Gauvinier? You called me, I believe.' He implied his time was a priceless asset about to be squandered. 'I really can't be too long.'

Gauvinier told him the story.

'. . . and this gives you eight hours tomorrow before the county *Times* goes to bed to verify our facts and build up the story. It also gives you twenty-four hours to line up the *Bugle* for the national splash that we're after.'

Jess interjected. 'Let's be quite frank with you, Mr Renton. If you do us proud then the rest of the story's yours, exclusive, for as long as it runs. We need you, and you need us. I'm quite willing to be used – all of us are – to build up the campaign. Our object is to stop the scheme from going ahead, at any cost.'

Renton grinned. 'You mean you don't care if I play it dirty so long as you win?'

Fanshawe started to protest, but Gauvinier hushed him with a raised hand. 'No, Oliver, he's right. Beeston will stab anyone in the back to get his own way, and he'll have no hesitation in trampling on any of us.'

Renton had crinkly light brown hair which backed away from his forehead in a series of tight wavelets. It was as if he kept it in curlers. He knew what he wanted.

'What's it worth to me?' he demanded.

'All the lineage you can make, you little hick,' said Jess nastily. Renton smiled back at him.

'Hack, you mean, I think. But what guarantee have I got that you'll keep the story exclusively for me? A guy can't live for ever on one hand-out. And Beeston's just bought the county *Times* group. I'm hardly going to be his blue-eyed boy when one of his own newspapers springs his own best-kept secret. I'll tell you what you can do. Make me your PR consultant. Fifty pounds a month plus expenses. Cash. I'll be reasonable.'

'Done,' said Jess before Fanshawe or anyone else could object. 'I'll guarantee the cash. It'll be worth the expense. Every PR man I've ever met who's worth his salt is a shit, and Mr Renton here qualifies. Sorry, vicar.'

'Not at all, Albert. My sentiments exactly.'

'Well, that's settled,' said Renton briskly, ignoring the insult. 'Then this is what I suggest we should do first . . .'

And so the 'Save Tillingfold' campaign was officially formed. Two days later, under Renton's by-line, the county *Times* carried a full two columns on the front page, headed: 'SHOCK PLAN FOR THIRTY MILLION POUND DEVELOPMENTS AT TILLINGFOLD', together with an artist's impression of the new complex and a statement from the Superstores Development Corporation saying that the natural beauty and historic atmosphere would not be damaged, but even enhanced, by the acquisition of seven acres of supermarkets and a further ten acres of tarmacadam parking space (free, to attract the customers), a new access road linking the village with the motorway from London and even (this would be phase II) a heliport to bring customers direct from Europe. Sir Philip Beeston, unfortunately, was absent from the country on holiday at the moment, and so was unavailable for comment.

Renton filed simultaneously a story for the *Bugle*, but was not unduly concerned that it never appeared. As an ambitious provincial journalist he was well acquainted with the vagaries of national news editors, and the fact that a particularly spectacular kidnapping occurred on the previous day meant that the entire attention of Fleet Street and the national radio and television news services was diverted accordingly. He had plenty of ammunition in his locker, so he bided his time. Meanwhile, he spent £15 of his new expense account on a meal at Tyling Manor, complete with a bottle of Nuits St George. He asked the manager to share his rather lonely bottle with him and was amply rewarded for his vicarious generosity.

Although the revelations of the prospective Tillingfold developments, therefore, rang no bells and raised no eyebrows on a national scale, the reactions within the village itself, and among various circles of local government leading right up to the Chairman of West Sussex County Council himself, were sufficiently animated to gratify the most avid of scandalmongers. The county *Times* sold out its entire edition and was obliged to print two thousand extra copies, unprecedented since the Acid Bath Murders were discovered in the district. It was naturally the supreme topic of conversation within Tillingfold itself, and opinion in the Dog and Duck, the Golden Hind and the Red Lion was sharply divided. By and large the Dog and Duck and the Golden Hind came down on the side of the traditionalists who were shocked and horrified by the plan; while the customers of the Red Lion, who on the whole averaged fifteen to twenty years fewer than those of the other two pubs, welcomed anything that smacked of progress. But opinions were by no means unanimous, and there was a sharp division for example between the saloon and the public bars of the Dog and Duck, where Gauvinier heard Paul White in 'the public' holding forth rather loudly about 'those old buggers being dragged kicking and screaming into the twentieth century' and took the opportunity to call across the bar: 'All right for Sunday, Paul?', to which White, not at all abashed, shouted back 'Sure, Guv (his pet name for Gauvinier). Might as well enjoy it while we can, eh?' Gauvinier contented himself with 'It's early days yet,' and went back to his pint and a whisky which he had bought for Renton.

The journalist was pleased with himself. The county *Times* editor had given him *carte blanche* to stay with the story indefinitely, to study the village's reactions and to cover all developments. Even though the *Bugle* hadn't used his first story, he had persuaded the London news editor to assign him to watch developments. So with his commission from the campaign as well he was due to draw three sets of expenses for the same job, and a minimum of £50 on top, which, Renton felt, couldn't be bad.

He settled down shrewdly to milk every possible piece of

advantage he could from the situation. To Fanshawe, he set the dull but important task of searching out the legal position; the actual state of the planning applications, if any, possible lines of defence and attack. 'Nothing illegal, Mr Fanshawe, mind,' he admonished, to Fanshawe's indignation and Gauvinier's amusement. To Jess and the vicar was given the all-important task of fund-raising – 'using the sublime and the Gorblimey, as it were' – and Gauvinier was appointed public spokesman by virtue of his position as chairman of the appeal, captain of the cricket club, and the fact that Renton assessed Gauvinier as the one most likely to put over his case adequately, particularly on television.

'Nonsense, it won't come to that,' protested Gauvinier. 'In any case I've no desire to go on the box. I make my living writing for others to do just that.'

Renton grinned at him.

'If your campaign's going to succeed, you'll have to go on telly. If we can't interest the media, we don't stand a snowball's chance. It's no good having Mr Jess here – he's got the wrong image.' Jess nodded. 'He's right.' 'Mr Fanshawe's too serious, he'll want to explain everything exactly and he'll have run out of time before they've asked him the first question. The vicar will be doing plenty of that from the pulpit, I should think, and we'll get him quoted anyway. But you're the one who's going to pull in your real backing, the cricketers. You wait and see if I'm not right.'

He paused and looked quizzically at Gauvinier.

'And you've got the face for it. Interesting, but not too handsome. And you know enough about the box not to make a fool of yourself.'

'Well, thanks very much for the compliment,' said Gauvinier dryly, and put the conversation out of his mind. Campaign or no campaign, he wanted to get up to the club to check how Frank Hunter and his cronies were getting on with mowing the outfield for the President's game on Sunday. The wicket was left to Fanshawe, who had tended it with loving care since old Francis had died in the early fifties aged ninety-four. Frank was responsible for the outfield, but he was inclined to be erratic. Gauvinier walked down in the dusk and was relieved to hear the sound of a Land-Rover engine revving up as he approached the line of chestnut trees bordering the cricket field. Hunter was just finishing, and waved cheerfully as the Land-Rover swept past Gauvinier on its last circuit of the field. It towed an ancient invention which had once mown the grass behind a Shire horse going at a gentle trot. Three circulating sets of blades, each four feet wide and overlapping each other by a foot, cut a wide swathe unexpectedly close, leaving the clippings on the outfield. Gauvinier breathed in the unmistakable scent and looked round the ground with satisfaction as Hunter pulled the vehicle round behind the pavilion and switched off. He joined Gauvinier.

''Tis a good smell, Peter. Fresh mown grass. Nothing like it.'

'Nothing in the world. It's good here, Frank. We don't want to leave it.'

Hunter did not answer him. Gauvinier looked at him.

'Why, Frank, don't you agree with me?'

'Oh, yes, I do at that, Mr Gauvinier. But there's more to it than that,' Hunter replied slowly. 'We all on us got to make a living, an' that's not all that easy these days.'

'You mean, if this new scheme goes through, it'll be good for business?'

Hunter was uncomfortable.

'Well yes, it might be. You never can tell. But if they're goin' to spend thirty millions, there's sure to be some pickings for the locals.'

'Is that what you've been told, Frank? By whom? James Mitterman?'

'Well, Mr Gauvinier, he did say summat about it, but he said not to tell.'

'All right, Frank, I won't press you. But I shouldn't count your chickens, you know. There's a long way to go yet. I was hoping you'd join our campaign to stop the scheme. But I suppose if you think there's something in it for you, it's no use trying to persuade you.'

He hoped this didn't sound as bitter as it felt.

''Ten't too much to worry about, Mr Gauvinier. 'Tes only the cricket club and the football club, after all. Soon find another field for they.'

'Oh Frank, that's not the point. Cricket's been played on this field now for 140 years. It's part of our history. Our past. Can't you see how important that is? Can't you believe that this development will wreck the village. It'll never be the same again.'

His protests sounded hollow in his own ears.

''Tes all very well, Mr Gauvinier, for the likes of you. Mebbe the past does mean a lot. But what about the future, then? 'Tes more important my bairns be fed than a bloody owd cricket match be played, I can tell you.'

'Oh come off it, Frank. Your kids are nearly grown up, and your garage is worth a small fortune. It's the biggest for miles around. What more do you want from life? D'you want to see all this destroyed?'

He looked around the darkening field. The spire of Tillingfold Church rose above the trees to one side. The new beeches which had been planted to soften the council estate were beginning to grow, their fresh green foliage masking the raw brick. Opposite, the close-planted chestnuts loomed black in the dusk, with behind them to the south the line of the Downs humped against the purpling sky. Over the pavilion, to the west, the sky glowed with its unbelievable mixture of carmine, purple, mauve and even green. He looked back at Hunter, seeing the narrow eyes, the thin line of the mouth, and knew it was no use trying to appeal to sentiment there. He laughed off his own earnestness.

'I get worked up about things, Frank. Perhaps you're right. Maybe it isn't worth fighting for. Good night. See you on Sunday. And thanks for the work.'

'That's okay, Peter. See you Sunday. Should be a good match. Are they strong this year?'

'Oh yes, Frank. We're in for some chasing on Sunday, I'll be bound. Have to put your spinning boots on. 'Night.'

It was extraordinary, he thought, walking slowly home, how inarticulate he became when confronted with apparently simple arguments. He'd have to do better than this on television if it came to that. He was suddenly overwhelmed with self doubt. Was he right, or monumentally wrong, to try to stand in the way of progress, to prevent perfectly respectable citizens like Frank Hunter from making a few extra pounds – or even many extra pounds? Frank was perfectly harmless, even well-meaning. He'd never charged for mowing the cricket field, and he'd done it willingly for years. He played cricket as wholeheartedly as anyone. What had Gauvinier to offer that Hunter had not? Why should Fanshawe be right and Mitterman wrong? And what *was* so important about cricket? He could always play, if not for Tillingfold, for another village. Or one of the big London clubs – Southgate, for instance, who'd asked him years ago to join. In his mind, he leaned back on the tried and trusted friendships of so many years, on Fanshawe and Veyzey, Budgeon and Colonel Trine; there were others, too, Colin Verrall and even old Fred Bason and new Albert Jess and some of the youngsters like Norman Smith. Even Paul White, for all his lip, he'd be on the right side, when it really came down to it. Gauvinier felt better.

He kissed Polly firmly on the mouth. She looked at him inquiringly.

'What's up with you then?' Gauvinier was not usually demonstrative. 'Oh Lord, defences up. You're spoiling for a fight, aren't you? I know you. You're looking forward to it all, and to hell with the rest of us. Oh well, I suppose we'll survive.'

'You'll survive all right.' Gauvinier grinned and added seriously, 'But will Tillingfold? I've an idea that this is going to be the most important time of our lives. But there's something we've got to do before anything else.'

'What's that, Peter?'

'Beat the hell out of the President's XI on Sunday. Come on, race you to bed.'

He smacked her on the bottom and left his hand on her soft plumpness as they climbed the stairs together.

Chapter 6

'Heads.'

The thin sunlight caught the spinning coin as it rose and fell above the two men's heads. Gauvinier let it drop on to the damp pitch and smiled wryly.

'Heads it is. My first mistake of the day. What's your pleasure?'

John Spicer, captain of Billington, who was skippering the President's XI, knew the Tillingfold wicket of old. It was as immaculate a square of grass as could be found in any village, and many a town pitch in the county, and Oliver Fanshawe maintained it with the care of a doting mother. But any wicket, no matter how perfect, will play merry hell with the bounce of the ball when the sun comes out on it after a week of heavy showers. There was no doubt, he thought, that the ball would 'fizz' early on and ease up later in the day if the sun stayed out. In any case, with the atmosphere humid and heavy, the new ball would be bound to swing for the quicker bowlers.

'Well, Peter. We'll let you have first go on Oliver's wicket, I think.'

He and Gauvinier were old friends and rivals.

'Don't blame you.' Gauvinier made batting signs to his team, who were filling the time before the match with some gentle batting practice and some not-so-gentle fielding, which he was pleased to see. Apart from the Mitterman incident, which he thrust to the back of his mind, there had been a couple of chances missed the previous week, which was unusual. To emphasize the dictum 'dropped catches, lost matches' he had instituted a 'fines' box for various misdemeanours, misfielding, dropped catches, wides and no-balls. The unfortunate possessor of a 'duck' paid 5p, along with the lesser offences. A 'golden duck' – out first ball – was worth 10p, as was a dropped 'sitter' or a four through a fielder's legs. By September the box weighed surprisingly heavily, and the seven or eight pounds always gave the end-of-season party a good send-off. To spread some of the responsibility and relieve himself of continual nagging, the position of 'fines man' went round the team game by game; and they all entered into it with some spirit, making it a competition to see who could take the most for the box. There was great glee when Gauvinier was fined 10p for forgetting to bring the scorebook to an away game. As he'd been out first ball (10p), dropped a catch (10p) and misfielded a boundary (15p), it was quite an expensive match . . . But the result of this good-natured discipline was a better turned-out team (5p for dirty boots or unpressed trousers) and a smarter fielding side than most. 'Always a pretty slippy lot at Tillingfold. They don't let many chances go a-begging.'

'What's all this about you having to lose your ground, Peter?' Spicer asked as they strolled leisurely back to the pavilion. 'Read it in the paper.'

'Oh, nothing's settled yet, John. I can't see us giving up the ground without a fight. But there's more to it than that. If they're allowed to go ahead with this scheme it will finish Tillingfold, there's no doubt about that.'

'What do the locals think about it?'

'Well, I'm surprised. Quite a few think it's a good idea to bring ourselves up to date.'

'You can't stop progress, I suppose. But I'd be sorry to see cricket finish at Tillingfold. You'll find somewhere else, I suppose?'

'That's not the point. If you give away one thing, you open the floodgates. In the end Tillingfold will join up with Billington and then Raveley in one great conglomeration and there'll be nothing left of all this,' he gestured around, 'apart from old photographs.'

'You're right, Peter, even if you sound a bit over-pessimistic. If there's anything we can do, let me know. Spread the word around, you know. It can't do any harm.'

'Thanks John. That might be very useful. Good luck.'

'Good luck.'

Gauvinier remembered to have a word with the club's scorer, Bobby Bewers. A leading, if reluctant, member of the church choir, he had begged leave from matins this morning. When he'd asked Albert Jess as choirmaster he'd been told to see the vicar for permission. Mr Veyzey looked over his glasses: 'Give me one reason, young Bewers, why I should let you off, as you put it, on Sunday. I am also playing, but I can't desert the church. The cricket match will just have to wait.'

There was no confusion about priorities in Bobby's mind.

'Well, sir,' he replied. ''Fyou don't mind me saying so, you don't have to be there like me. If Guv, I mean Mr Gauvinier, wins the toss an' we bat, you won't be in first, an' if we field, they can send on a sub. But somebody's got to keep the score properly all the time.' He implied that there was no one in the village, from Mr Veyzey downwards, who was capable of doing the job as well as he. And, thought Veyzey, he was probably right. No one, that is, who would irradiate such patent enthusiasm and loyalty. The vicar cast a half-glance upwards, as if in apology.

'All right, Bobby, but on one condition.'

'What's that, sir?' Bobby was cautious. Experience had warned him that the vicar's 'quids' were often rather more expensive than his 'quos'.

'I'll be wanting "Oh for the Wings" the Sunday after next; it'll mean two extra practices. And no smoking.'

'Oh, all right.' The price was steep, but payable. Without thanking the vicar he shot out of the door like a stone from a catapult, leaving Veyzey to wonder why He who gave certain of His creatures voices like angels should so often select those whose appearance, character and behaviour resembled young imps of the Devil. He liked young Bobby, but he knew that the odds were heavy against his growing up to fulfil the expectations that shone in his eyes. Gauvinier too was aware of the problems confronting a lad of twelve whose father deserted his mother and six brothers and sisters after beating them all regardless of age or sex for the past thirteen years. The fact that Charlie Bewers had merely moved his clothes and his beery breath to the widow Telfer's, a couple of hundred yards away, and that in spite of everything Emily Bewers cried her eyes out for him every night was common knowledge. But only a few people, including Veyzey and Gauvinier and Thomas Pugh, the schoolmaster, recognized that under the veneer of cynicism and toughness Bobby Bewers carried with him as a shield, there was a wealth of romantic creativity struggling to emerge. The cricket club's score-book was almost a work of art.

'No slip-ups with the telegraph today,' Gauvinier adjured Bobby. 'Who've you got?'

'There's the Philips kid until dinner time, an' Jones an' the two little Smiths after.' Bobby was proud to be organizing for his hero. 'Don't you worry, Guv.'

Keeping the scoreboard going properly was one of those small efficiencies which made Tillingfold cricket known and respected for miles around. In the past two years, the old system of runs, wickets, last man had been revised and up-dated to show each batsman's score, and the score at the fall of the last wicket, as well as (for the second half of the match) the number of runs required to win and the number of overs left to be bowled in the last hour. As the batting side was often too busy, or not interested, in performing the necessary chore of altering the numbers constantly, Gauvinier had delegated the task to young Bewers to arrange. There were occasional flurries when his minions were too young to maintain their concentration or possibly even to reach the top line of protruding nails, but on the whole it worked well and the Tillingfold scoreboard was a constant talking-point.

'Well, James, you can take your time today. We've got all day to make the runs. If the weather lasts.'

Gauvinier worked enthusiasm into his voice for the benefit of his opening batsman, although he had little hope that it would spark Mitterman into playing anything like an innings. The accountant was standing now, methodically checking every item of equipment: boots, pads, thigh guard, 'box', bat, batting gloves, cap; all of which appeared to be brand-new. Even the straps on Mitterman's pads were clipped back so no flapping loose end might touch a ball and mislead an umpire into giving a catch at the wicket. The flat bland face gave nothing away. Gauvinier wondered what was going on in the mind behind it. Was Mitterman thinking of the wicket, the innings to come, the speed of the bowlers, the weather?

'I'm well aware of that, Peter, thank you. I shall do my best, as always.'

'So much for me,' thought Gauvinier, but at this stage of the game his anticipation was such that his armour was impenetrable, and he turned to grin and applaud as Mitterman and Jess strode out together to open the innings, an incongruous pair if ever there was one.

Mitterman, indeed, was doing his best to concentrate. He had learned a great deal in forty-odd years of survival on his wits. Among the lessons he had ingested was the fact that if you wish to deceive others the only person you must never fool is yourself. He had not, therefore, deluded himself into believing that he was a good cricketer. He recognized that his co-ordination was poor, that he had little sense of timing and even that he was (slightly but effectively) frightened of the hardness of a cricket-ball. The thing he did not understand was why, knowing all this, he still wished to make his mark in the village through the cricket club and expended much money and energy in trying to do so. He had a healthy respect (in cricket terms) for natural games players like Gauvinier and Jess, who had an affinity with the moving ball that he knew he could never possess.

As he took guard and carefully made his mark, one part of his mind was on what his coach at the Gover school had told him: 'Don't *grasp* the handle, hold it naturally. Watch the bowler all the way. Left elbow up a bit. Watch the ball.' The bowler ran up tidily, holding the ball low in his right hand, his fingers pointing to the ground. Mitterman shifted his feet a little. Suddenly, in a flurry of action, whirlwind arms and legs, the ball was at him and past him, a red flash wide of the off-stump, before he could move his bat. He heard the ball thump into the wicket-keeper's gloves and breathed a little more easily. The next four balls were wide outside the off-stump too, and he began to realize that in the heavy atmosphere the bowler was swinging the ball too early and too far to trouble him. The trembling in his knees quietened and he was able to meet the last ball of the over, which was slower and straighter, moving his left leg down the pitch towards the bowler and playing the ball towards the bottom of his bat some eight inches away from his pad.

The bowler, seeing the gap between bat and pad, made a mental note to try to get one to cut in towards the wickets from the off. Mitterman, grateful for lasting six balls without disaster, leaned on his bat as he remembered seeing Sir Len Hutton doing at Lord's. He wondered where the wicket would come on the Beeston development plan. Probably right at the front entrance to Tesco's, he thought. He was recalled from such unprofitable speculation by Fanshawe, in his umpire's capacity, asking him to 'Move over, please, James.' The new bowler wanted to bowl 'left arm over the wicket', which meant that Mitterman, as the non-striking batsman, would have to move to the other side of the crease.

At the other end of the wicket Jess, his crumpled flannels and pads worn to an indeterminate grey, presented a contrast to the immaculate Mitterman. Small, neat in action but invariably untidy in dress, Jess spent his time between balls practising his strokes, like a golfer before driving. Mitterman tried not to let the constant movement rattle him, but he was vulnerable, as he admitted, to distractions. Jess, on the other hand, was so wrapped up in his cricket that he hardly knew he was fidgeting at all. It was the same in the field. While Jess was like a cat on hot bricks, constantly jigging around, stretching his muscles, dashing to back up for other fielders' throwing, Mitterman stood ponderous and immobile, as if uninterested. While batting, Mitterman took guard with enormous care, moving his bat fractionally to the umpire's directions until he was absolutely sure that 'Middle, inclined to leg', which he affected, had been achieved. Then, with precision, he would scratch a line in the turf with the toe stud of his right boot, and finally hammer his block-hole at exactly forty-five degrees. He was quite put out if (as rarely happened) he were to survive his partner and other batsmen arrived at the crease whose marks tended to obscure his, holding up the game for long minutes while he re-took his guard and went through the whole rigmarole again. Gauvinier reckoned that Mitterman was worth as much in nuisance value as he was in runs, although to the batting side from the pavilion watching Mitterman was a trial in itself.

Jess, on the other hand, had no mind for style or appearances. He took his guard with a quick pat of the bat. 'Leg stump, umpire . . .' 'A shade to you . . .' 'Oh, that'll do . . .' Strangely, his runs came much as Mitterman's did, behind the bat, although Jess's were often intentional whereas Mitterman's were merely gifts from fortune. Now, facing the gentleman bowling left arm over, Jess seemed to Mitterman to be enviably at ease. His bat came down in a slow arc, arriving with quite ridiculous smoothness at the same time as the ball, steering it rather than hitting it down to fine leg, where a fielder had a long chase, enabling the batsmen to make two runs. The next ball Jess was a pace down the wicket when he met the ball, deflecting it wide of second slip from a very thick edge, for an easy single down to the third man. Now Mitterman went through his pantomime again, taking guard, and facing the new bowler with trepidation and defiance emanating from him in equal quantities. 'Poor old

James,' thought Gauvinier. 'It won't bite him.' It did the next best thing. The ball's swing, through his half-defensive prod, rapped Mitterman hard and high on the fleshy part of the inside right thigh, missing pad and thighguard alike. Mitterman dropped his bat and doubled over, rubbing his leg vigorously.

It was only a temporary respite, however, and soon, with the soreness from his inner thigh spreading to his groin, he was facing up to the left-hander again. This time he stabbed spitefully at the ball to some purpose, getting an inside edge as it swung in again towards him. The ball snicked like lightning between bat and pad, beating wicket and keeper alike, speeding towards the boundary for four runs, the first boundary of the innings.

'Well placed, sir.' Frank Hunter's cheery laugh echoed across the ground from the pavilion, where the President's first half-barrel of beer had been breached and was already flowing freely. 'They all look the same in the book.'

Gauvinier reflected that the clichés of village cricket were probably equivalent to those in any society – obscure, obsolete or at best obsolescent, and incomprehensible to all but the initiated. Yet he found himself using them with quiet enjoyment as in the companionship of old friends. It was at least consoling to know that millions of Americans used the phrase 'it isn't cricket' for bad sportsmanship without having the slightest notion of what a cricket bat was or half an inkling of the weight and consistency of a cricket ball.

Meanwhile Mitterman scored another run, this time off a nasty lifting ball that hit his thumb and shot away to leg, and Jess had put ten up on the board with a late cut for two, uppishly but safely past second slip's grasping right hand.

'Over ball,' called Fanshawe, and marched firmly to square-leg and the left-arm bowler retired to the deep field, aggrieved that his best ball, the one that should have taken a wicket, had been snicked to the boundary by a tyro, and that second slip hadn't made a greater effort to catch the batsman, the scruffy little one whose shirt was coming out of his trousers and down his backside.

Gauvinier, for whom ten on the board was a small landmark which eased slightly his ever-present misgivings about Tillingfold's batting stability, sniffed the air and decided that the meteorological forecasters were right and it would probably rain later on. As he pulled out a deck-chair and settled down to watch, he saw a new Jaguar convertible pull off the road and swing out of sight behind the pavilion wall. A hand waved from the passenger window and he waved back, wondering who had come into a fortune. He did not know the driver. He watched Jess coping capably with Hatch, the near-county standard right-hand bowler, for a couple of balls, and felt the sun reappear from behind the clouds, which seemed to be beginning to lift and break up as they lifted over the Downs from the south-west.

He felt hands on the back of his deck-chair.

''Morning, Peter. There's someone I want you to meet.'

Gauvinier twisted around, none too eagerly. Above his head, half-watching the play, was Renton. With him was a small, brown-faced man with a balding head, extending a thin hand.

'Alex Wheel, meet Peter Gauvinier, Tillingfold's skipper. Alex gave me a lift over, Peter. He said he wanted to meet you. He's from the *Bugle*. You know . . .'

Alex Weighall, pronounced Wheel, was Fleet Street's most quoted sports writer, Columnist of the Year. Gauvinier shook the proffered hand.

'Pleased to meet you. Nice of you to come down. Renton, get a couple more chairs, would you mind?' It was not often Gauvinier 'pulled rank', but he had decided he did not like Phillip Renton. The Fleet Street man smiled to himself. He liked men who knew their own minds.

'I don't want to distract you from your game, Mr Gauvinier,' he began, as he settled himself in the low deck-chair with some discomfort. 'It's just that I think you've a story here, and I want to get it right. If I could just sit here and sort of absorb a Sunday on the village green, I'll be quite happy. I like cricket, you know. Used to play it myself once. Not to any effect,' he added deprecatingly.

Gauvinier warmed to him. This wasn't the usual hustling whizz-kid.

'If you really want to stick around and find out what's happening, you're welcome,' he said. 'Why don't you come to lunch with us? Renton will have told you it's the President's match today, and we're all going down to the village hall for beer and bangers. You'll get all the atmosphere you want.'

'That's really most accommodating of you,' Weighall said. 'I've got all day. I won't disturb you, but if you'd oblige me by filling in the gaps in Renton's story, I'd be obliged.' He tapped the copy of the county *Times* he was carrying. 'I've already questioned him, of course, but his view's inclined to be, er, professional. I won't quote you if you don't want to be quoted. I don't know if you've read any of my stuff.'

Gauvinier had indeed, as had any sportsman in Britain who enjoyed good writing. Weighall had discovered a style of sports reporting somewhere between the hard news, angle-ridden abruptness of the tabloids and the esoteric ramblings of the 'quality' press. His writing was hard-hitting, occasionally vitriolic, and articulate. He quoted no one, and hid behind no one's skirts, stating his own opinions and backing them up with sometimes unexpected arguments. His editor gave him more and more space to the envy of his colleagues and the hatred of his rivals, some of whom tried without success to match him. He wrote only when he wanted to and what he chose to write. If he was on your side, he could do a great deal for your cause. If against, equally he could ruin you. His paper sold five million copies a day, and he was paid a small fortune.

Gauvinier took a chance.

'Look,' he said, watching Jess take a quick single. 'I'm biased in all this. Why don't you dig around from scratch and see what you come up with. I wouldn't want to influence you – or rather, I would, but it might work the wrong way.'

'Fair enough,' said Weighall. 'But I've got to start somewhere, and I might as well begin with you. You know all about what's going on.'

'Indeed I don't.' He paused to clap a well-hit three runs. 'No, that's enough,' he called. 'You know, our running isn't all it could be sometimes. Sorry, where was I? Oh, yes, I know. Well, we're not very clear ourselves what we're up against yet. All we really know is what's in the paper. The man who can help you is Mitterman – he's out there batting at the moment. He's something to do with the Superstore's plan, but what, he hasn't been good enough to tell us yet.'

'You mean, you haven't asked him? And he hasn't volunteered anything?'

Gauvinier was embarrassed.

'Well, this all came out on Friday, and we haven't had time to assess it all yet. This is a cricket club, not a barber's shop.'

Weighall went up a couple of notches in Gauvinier's estimation by fielding the inference neatly.

'But you still gossip, don't you? There's not a village in Britain where this sort of thing doesn't get talked about, and Tillingfold's no different from any other, I'll warrant.'

'Well, possibly I could have got him to talk but we're not quite on speaking terms at the moment,' Gauvinier said reluctantly. 'We had a bit of a tiff last week – nothing important – but James and I have only exchanged formalities since then.'

Weighall made a mental note, and let the matter pass over. He'd know all about this within an hour or two. He moved on.

'What are you going to do?'

'I don't know there's much we can do, apart from get you chaps interested. We'll make an official protest, through the club, to the planning people, but we don't have much hope there. I expect James and his friends will have the official channels sewn up. No, I think that public opinion's the only way. If we can build up enough head of steam we can maybe force a public inquiry.'

They sat and watched the slow progress of the game for a spell, thinking. Weighall spoke thoughtfully.

'You have one enormous advantage, if you can mobilize it.'

'What's that?'

'Cricket itself. If you can get other cricketers on your side, you could go a long way. The hold cricket has on the people who run this country is quite astonishing – even the House of Commons runs a cricket team. Badly, of course, as is to be expected. The Duke himself plays. I think you'd be amazed at the support you'd find.'

'You mean we should contact every cricket club? There must be thousands. It'd cost a packet.'

'Not if you found a printer who was a cricketer willing to help— Oh lor', you've lost a wicket.'

'Blast it, so we have. That was a good shot too – bad luck, Albert. Well played.'

This to the departing batsman, who was returning from the crease taking off his batting gloves and looking ruefully at the ground as the small smattering of applause rang out.

'Thirty-one for one, last man twenty-three,' the treble of Bobby Bewers came from the scorebox window.

'That was a bit of shrewd captaincy,' Gauvinier observed to his guest. 'You don't often see two backward short legs in this class of game.'

His rival, noting that Jess favoured the leg glance, and that the wicket was 'holding up' the ball, had brought up his deep fine leg fieldsman into a wide leg slip position, and moved square leg finer, at the same time bringing mid-on in to the 'silly' position, forming a perfect leg trap for his left-hander to bowl to. Jess, tied down by some accurate bowling, eventually tried to sweep a ball that lifted a little and shot very fast off the edge of his bat to leg slip, where the fielder, after some juggling in front of his body, held the catch. Gauvinier called 'Good luck, Fred,' to the incoming batsman, Bason, who made his way with massive tread to the wicket. The bat looked like a matchstick in his hand.

'What's he like?' Weighall asked Gauvinier.

'Oh, Fred's a steady cricketer, but when he gets a loose ball he can hit it. Like that. Look out!'

Fred had thumped his first ball, a full toss, right over the close field and it was racing straight for them with not a fieldsman in sight. Applause rang out for the four and silly mid-on decided that the position really was foolish and moved back a yard or so more from the batsman. Weighall bent down in his chair to field the ball as it ran across the whitewashed boundary line and tossed it back to mid-off, who had made a long chase for nothing.

'First time I've touched a ball in years. It takes me right back. Now, can you fill me in about the background to the club?'

At that moment a concerted shout rang out from the field as the bowler, wicket-keeper and slips all appealed for a catch at the wicket. Slowly, deliberately, Fanshawe's finger went up. Fred Bason was out off his second ball for four runs. Thirty-five for two wickets.

Gauvinier rose.

'I must go and pad up. Never do for the captain to be late on parade. If you'll excuse me. Fanshawe's the man to talk to about Tillingfold's history. He's the umpire this end. Have a chat with him over lunch, if you've time to stay.'

'I've all the time in the world. I'm beginning to enjoy this. The pace is a bit different from Lord's. More happens in less time. Don't mind me. You just carry on. I'll talk to Mr Fanshawe later.'

Gauvinier, relieved, watched the number four batsman, White, reach the crease, take guard, and block his first ball competently. He did not like to talk much during a match, even on so important a topic. He liked his mind and energies to be concentrated on the game itself, which he found all-absorbing. He had forgotten about Weighall and Superstores by the time he had fastened on his first pad. Like many cricketers, Gauvinier was slightly superstitious, and he always strapped his pads on left one first, and from the bottom strap upwards. It was a routine started thirty years ago when he was at school, and it was invariable. If he was interrupted or for any reason jogged out of the sequence, he felt uncomfortable, as if he'd forgotten something. Although to be honest he'd always forgotten about it before he got to the wicket, and he never knew if the ritual made any difference to his batting. He removed his sweater. That was another superstition. He did not like having to take it off out in the middle after he'd warmed up and was sweating. It involved holding up the game, removing his batting gloves, rolling up his sleeves and generally destroying his concentration at the wicket. So unless the day was bitterly cold, he always went out to bat in shirt sleeves.

He expected to be batting quite soon, for he had little faith in Mitterman's ability either to stay at the crease or to score runs. But today, some imp of fortune had given Mitterman a charmed life. While White played himself in competently at the other end, Mitterman prodded and poked his way into double figures and then, slowly, towards the twenties. True, one ball shot off the shoulder of his bat and fell just over first slip's head and he got a run instead of being caught. He survived confident appeals for l.b.w. at both ends. His inner thigh smarted and the pain shot up into his groin when he set off on a run. But, limping and perspiring, he survived and the runs began to come off both inner and outer edges of his bat.

There is nothing more exasperating (except a last-wicket stand) to a bowler than a batsman who, though clearly incompetent and his natural victim, manages to stay at the wicket, *and* score runs. Spicer, the visiting captain, felt the same, and kept his opening bowlers on too long in the conviction that one or other of them *must* take Mitterman's wicket at any moment. A faint flush began to tinge Mitterman's usually pale cheeks; after each run he was forced to remove his cap and wipe the perspiration from his brow. After the second l.b.w. appeal was turned down he actually took off his sweater and handed it to the umpire. He forgot Superstores quite early on, and began to lose his fear of the ball. On one occasion he even put his left foot down the pitch and drove the ball past cover point for two runs. It was unprecedented.

'D'you know, I think the blighter's enjoying himself?' Gauvinier, leaning against the pavilion door, spoke to himself, and looked round a little guiltily to see if he'd been overheard. Bason winked at him.

Together, the third wicket put on thirty more runs, but it was too good to last. Spicer, giving in at last, changed the bowling and brought on a middle-aged off-spinner who regularly took his fifty wickets a season for a club just outside Brighton. Mitterman, bewildered by the spinning ball, tried to fend it off cross-batted as it came into his body from the off, and swatted a simple catch back to the bowler. He departed, collecting his sweater from the visiting umpire on the way, to receive genuine, as opposed to the usual merely sympathetic, applause. He had scored twenty-four.

'Well done, James,' Gauvinier slapped him on the shoulder as he lumbered, panting slightly, through the pavilion door. 'That was a good knock.'

'Ah, but I had quite a bit of luck,' Mitterman was suitably modest. 'I knew what to do with the quickies, but I haven't any idea how to cope with the spinners.'

'We'll get Fred to tweak some at you in the nets,' said Gauvinier. 'Oh, Lord.'

As a prayer it might have been more suitable for the vicar, the new batsman, who had tried to cut Vines, the off-spinner, off his first ball and had been neatly and easily caught at first slip. 'We could have done without that.'

'Seventy-one, four, nought,' called Bobby. 'Put the duck up this time.'

The placing of the little duck in place of the 'o' for a batsman who was so unfortunate as 'not to trouble the scorers' had grown in Tillingfold to be something of an honour, though it might conceivably have been regarded as a left-handed compliment. You had to have earned a 'duck' either by long service to the club or by some special circumstance. The self-appointed custodian of the unwritten custom was Bobby Bewers, who at the age of twelve had an instinctive knowledge of what was right and what was wrong, just as his predecessors had, for the past seventy years. The vicar was certainly in the 'duck' category.

Gauvinier, facing the task of preventing the hat-trick, was

apprehensive. He knew Vines of old to be an excellent bowler who could be deadly when the wicket was in his favour. As he strolled to the wicket, he was calculating deliberately on his methods of defence. If he played forward, he would obviate most of the chance of being l.b.w., but at the same time would leave himself vulnerable if the ball was to 'pop' on the uncertain wicket. If he played back, he might easily be trapped by the swiftly turning ball. He decided to leave it to his natural reactions, and not, at all costs, to have a swipe.

While he took guard (a careful 'Two legs, please') Spicer, the opposing captain, was bringing up his forces in search of the bowler's greatest prize, the third wicket in three balls. Eight fielders and the wicket-keeper ringed Gauvinier, none of them further than ten yards from the bat. One man patrolled the covers thirty yards away, the eleventh man, of course, being Vines the bowler. He appeared unmoved by his opportunity. He watched Gauvinier settle in to his crease, strolled back to his mark, turned casually and ambled in, bringing his arm over in the action he'd performed a hundred thousand times before.

Gauvinier watched the ball floating through the air towards him, red and shiny as if it were in slow motion. He could see it spinning in flight, swinging slightly away from him. It was well pitched up, he thought, on a length. He pushed his left leg forward down the pitch, the bat alongside it, towards the pitch of the ball. His bat was angled forward, his wrists limp, the model of a forward defensive stroke as taught in the cricket schools. The ball dipped early, pitched and turned sharply past his left elbow. There was a click and the noise of movement behind him as the wicket-keeper removed the bails, a vast shout of 'Howzzatt!' from eleven concerted throats. Gauvinier, stranded on his forward foot, looked towards the square leg umpire. Fanshawe's finger was up. Gauvinier looked back at his right foot. The toe of his boot was resting on the white popping crease. 'The line is mine . . .': the old wicket-keeper's axiom. He was out.

'Well bowled. Superb.' No one spared a thought for Gauvinier as, with a heart-felt 'Well bowled, Tony,' he left the wicket. The fielders clustered round Vines, shaking his hand, clapping him on the back. Generous applause from the batting side issued from the direction of the pavilion. The wicket-keeper, grinning from ear to ear and unable to stand still in his delight, strolled up to the group round Vines, tossing the ball from one red-palmed glove to the other. Vines broke through the congratulatory circle and clasped him, football-wise, round the waist. The two experienced and normally composed cricketers performed a little jig together. 'Brilliant stumping, brilliant,' they all cried, and Aloysious Dewbury, Raveley's black wicket-keeper imported for the match, grinned as though his face would break in half. A leg-side stumping is the acme of the wicket-keeper's art, and Dewbury had performed this one with a slickness and timing rarely seen at village level.

As Gauvinier neared the pavilion, the schoolboy, Alan Haynes, stood up and the figures seventy-one, five, duck went up on the scoreboard. Gauvinier checked the new man in. 'Wait a minute, Alan, is Teddy ready?'

'Ready and willing, skip.' Trine, eager for a knock, was always padded up well in advance even of Gauvinier's maxim that batsmen should be padded up two wickets in advance.

'Out you go, Teddy, and take care.'

'OK, skip, leave it to me.' Gauvinier wished he had Trine's confidence in his own ability. He was taking a chance that Trine's genial insensitivity would make light of the suddenly heavy atmosphere and parlous state of Tillingfold's innings. He disliked changing the order of batting at the last moment, for it meant that someone's nose was put out of joint, but young Haynes, after looking slightly crestfallen, was also quite relieved to be taken out of the firing line at a critical juncture. Gauvinier, thanking him, reflected that in any future war valour would come much harder, and therefore be more meritorious to Haynes than to Trine. Haynes would torture himself with self-doubt before going into action, while Trine would cheerfully win a VC before breakfast without giving the consequences a second thought.

Gauvinier walked through the deck-chairs to a chorus of 'hard luck', 'not to worry, Guv' and 'our turn'll come' and turned to watch the remainder of Vines's over before taking off his pads. Once more the nine men crouched around the batsman as Vines swung in to bowl in complete silence. Trine placed a long leg down the wicket, swung his bat, and the funereal atmosphere shattered as the ball swung into the chestnut trees for a six amid shouts and cheers from the batting side. The fieldsmen retreated into more prudent positions as Trine treated the next ball in the same way, clearing the trees this time and landing in the fall full pitch in the village pond across the road. The last ball of the over he swung at again, and it sliced off the bat over gulley's head and ran down to the boundary for four runs amid laughter and more cheers.

Frank Hunter, furious that Trine had been preferred to him to break the spell of Vines, thought that some people had all the luck and glared at Gauvinier. Gauvinier, who had moments of total insight, grinned back at him and said: 'Some people have all the luck, don't they, Frank?' to which Hunter managed a noise like 'tcchk' and sucked his cheeks in knowingly, nodding his head and casting his eyes to heaven simultaneously. The vicar, emerging smiling from the dressing-room, said, as if making a profound observation from the pulpit: 'Wicket, wicket, wicket. Six, six, four. A remarkable over.' To which Gauvinier could think of nothing more original to say than 'You don't say, Reverend. What on earth's happened now?'

For the players were straggling from the field, opening a gap to let the batsmen through to a little routine of hand-clapping. The umpires removed the bails from the stumps and followed in, with the measured tread of umpires the world over, and Gauvinier, after checking for rain, realized that in the swift passage of time lunch was upon them. He hastened to make sure Weighall and Renton were included, but Renton excused himself on the grounds that his paper needed him.

'Watch that young man,' Weighall said reflectively to Gauvinier.

'We'd already formed that opinion. But why, particularly?'

'He's greedy. He'll do you down at the drop of an expenses sheet.'

'He's been quite useful so far. But thanks for the warning. Why, by the way, should we have any more faith in you?'

Weighall smiled. Thirty years in journalism had taught him that taking offence was unproductive.

'I'm so well paid I don't have to fiddle my exes,' he replied calmly. 'But I don't mind a free beer when one's about to be offered.'

Gauvinier, chiding himself for his lack of hospitality, hastened to make amends, introducing Weighall to Colonel Trine en route.

'Colonel Trine, this is Alex Weighall, of the *Daily Bugle*. He's come to write us up. I'm just going to get him a beer.'

Weighall possessed an elephantine memory allied to a skill in identifying himself with whomsoever he was talking to, which, to him, meant interviewing.

'Colonel Trine? Palestine, wasn't it? Second Paras, Naharya, nineteen forty-eight? I remember you, but you wouldn't remember me. I was a squaddie doing my conscription . . .'

The Colonel shook him vigorously by the hand. 'Palestine, eh? Second Battalion? Good God, that brings back memories. You're most welcome Mr – er . . .?'

Weighall supplied the omission.

'Yes. Well, what can I do to help you? You're stopping for a bite of lunch, I hope. This is my day – President's match and all that. My son's playing. Just hit a couple of sixes, eh? He's over there. Teddy, come and meet the man from Fleet Street. You can fill him in with all the details.'

'Righto, father.' He shook hands with Weighall. 'I don't know if I can be of much help.'

'Oh, come off it, Teddy.' The Colonel bent his moustache towards Weighall's ear. 'His firm's right in the thick of the whole damned business.' His voice carried obvious disapproval. Weighall waved his hand airily to Edward.

'Don't worry about me. I'm not on duty today. I've come to

watch a game of cricket – and have some more of that excellent beer. What is it? Local brew?'

'Yes, it's from Horsham. Let me fill you up again.'

'I'll be nodding off and missing all the interesting bits.'

'Oh, so you are on duty after all? When does the inquisition begin?'

'Only when you're ready for it. May I come to your office tomorrow? Is it in Tillingfold or Billington? Or Horsham?'

'Do you mind? Nothing so classy as that. I'm the local chap. Director they call it, but if you ask for the office boy you get me too. Just up the High Street on the left. Handsome and Wellbeloved.'

'I beg your pardon?'

'Handsome and Wellbeloved. It's a branch of Sibling and Sibling, the national estate agents. We're handling the negotiations for the land. I really can't tell you very much. It'd be more than my life's worth. But come and have a cup of coffee tomorrow morning by all means. Are you staying down overnight?'

'Yes, I thought I might. It'll save running back to Buckinghamshire.'

'Try Tyling Manor. They run about a dozen rooms and I happen to know there's a double free. Someone cried off. The manager's a pal of mine and he was quite put out when I was over there last night. Here's the number.'

He dug in his blazer pocket and came up with a dozen or so visiting cards. He extracted one and gave it to Weighall.

'Tyling Manor,' it read. 'Luncheon, dinners and accommodation. Telephone Tillingfold 243.' And below, discreetly: 'E. R. Trine'.

'You get around, Mr Trine. How many other interests have you?'

'Nothing to do with me. Not on merit, anyway,' Trine laughed modestly. 'Well, the local chaps seem to want the name Trine on their boards, and it adds to the coffers. I do a bit for Christie's now and then, if I come across any loot tucked away in cobwebby cupboards – on commission, of course. And I'm on the board of Bason's Builders – Fred over there's the boss. The Guv'nor thinks I'm idling my life away, but I'm really quite energetic. If this thing comes off I shall be able to restore the family fortunes quite a bit – get back the Goya he had to sell to keep me at Marlborough and that sort of thing. I'd never have got to Oxford under my own steam, you know.'

'Will it worry you if it doesn't come off?'

'Oh, I don't suppose so,' said Trine carelessly. 'Plenty of other fish in the pond. Or used to be, I suppose. Why d'you ask?'

'Well, would you be interested if there was anything crooked in the deal?'

'How d'you mean? Dodging the tax man, and all that?'

'Well, that and worse. Try bribery, for one.'

Trine took a long pull at his beer.

'I've never really thought about it,' he said with the air of one who has just made an unexpected discovery. 'I don't mind bucking the tax man – everyone's doing that all the time. But anything *illegal*, no. I draw the line there.' He looked at Weighall suspiciously.

'You're not writing that this deal has a seamy side, are you? It's all straightforward development. The village needs it, and it's going to get it.'

'Even if it costs all this.' Weighall swept an arm around much as Gauvinier had done on the previous Friday night.

'Oh, there's nothing so precious in all this. My father thinks I'm a heretic, we should maintain our standards and all that bullshit. But Fred Bason and I have already got our eye on an alternative field; and we'll pay for the square and build a new pavilion – the lot.'

'Doesn't it worry you when you're going out to bat?'

'Good Lord, no. Why should it? A short life and a merry one, that's my motto. If we all spent the time worrying about destroying the past we'd never even get round to enjoying the present.'

'Or looking to the future? Your skipper seems to feel very strongly about it. And no doubt others feel the same way.'

'Old Guv? I suppose he does. But he'll get used to it. He'll have to, won't he?'

'Why should he? He'll fight, anyhow.'

'It won't do him much good. We'll win, of course.'

'Why do you think that? It might not be such a pushover.'

'Oh, you can't beat the sort of money that's going into this thing. Old Mitterman knows which side his bread's buttered on. Sir Thingummy Whatsisname doesn't back losers.'

Alex Weighall, in the words of his trade, got around. He was by no means the columnist blinkered to the exclusion of the rest of the world. He knew a thing or two about Sir Philip Beeston.

'Perhaps not. But he sometimes buys the losers before the race.'

Trine flushed. 'Look, I don't give a damn what you think about Beeston. He's been straight with us over this deal, and the deal's straight too. Our firm, well, Sibling and Sibling, wouldn't have anything to do with it if it were crooked. They've got a national reputation to keep up. Anyway my bosses have a great deal of respect for Beeston.'

'So they should, young man. I happened to notice a small financial report on one of Superstores' holding companies the other day. You know who actually owns Sibling and Sibling? Yes, you're right. Sir Philip Beeston. God bless his little cotton socks.'

'How the devil do you know?'

'Oh, I know all right. I know something else that you don't, too. Sir Philip Beeston owns the *Bugle*, too. So he's my ultimate boss as well as yours, and Renton's over there.'

'Good God. Doesn't that inhibit you on this sort of a thing?'

'Oh, I don't think so. I'm like your skipper.' He nodded towards Gauvinier. 'I like a scrap too.'

They walked across the field and up the High Street to the village hall, where white-suited tables were laid with plates of ham, salad and new potatoes, with strawberries and cream afterwards. Two more 'polypins' of beer stood ready breached for the thirsty guests (about three pints each, when you subtracted the teetotallers). Gauvinier, still smarting from his 'duck', permitted himself two pints and a 'top up', arguing that the President's match only happened once a season, and it was the only time he broke his rule of not drinking during a match. On tour, that was different, and he umpired the club six-a-side competition with a pint mug on the grass behind the stumps. If anyone spilled it, he had to re-fill it. But he drew the line at smoking on the field at any time.

Lunch was companionable, and genial, and went on too long. And by a quarter to three Tillingfold were batting again, somewhat hazily, to bowling from which much of the sting had been removed by liberal doses of best bitter. Even Gauvinier found difficulty in concentrating on the cricket, and was forced to stand up and stroll round the boundary to 'work off' the after-effects of a full stomach and the stupor imposed by Colonel Trine's cliché-ridden speech. Gauvinier, not for the first time, wished that army training included a course on public speaking. Trine, blissfully impervious, had rambled on.

'Stop me if you've heard this one before. An Irishman went into a bar . . . for Peter Gauvinier, who does so much for the club . . . he won't *duck out* of anything (heavy emphasis: laughter and applause) . . . Tillingfold tangled in the Vines (more laughter) . . . but young Tony there (more laughter: Tony Vines was fifty-three, the oldest man on the field) . . . have to catch a Trine.' The Colonel sat down beaming and chuckling to himself at his closing pun, mopping his brow and pouring himself a brandy from a silver flask he pulled from a capacious inside pocket of his tweed jacket.

'Run up . . .' Gauvinier was surprised to realize that the bellowed instruction breaking in on his thoughts was his own. White, who had been batting steadily, if without inspiration, had hit the ball nicely into the covers, well to the left hand of Slater, the coverpoint, and stood hesitating a third of the way down the pitch. 'No – wait – *No*!' The final decisive command stopped Trine, who looked as though he might be going to break into a canter, in his tracks, and sent him scampering back to the bowler's crease, easily beating Slater's rather wide throw. 'We won't put up much of a score if we don't take what's offered,' Gauvinier thought testily.

Out in the middle Paul White waved an apology. 'Sorry, Teddy, there was one there.'

'Not to worry, old son. Are you all right?' with quick anxiety.

'Just a bit out of breath. It'll pass.'

He settled down for his next ball. He could feel the tightness in his chest and absurdly breathless feeling as his body tried to evade the annoying little tickle which occurred in his chest at the end of every breath. He'd had it some time now, a subterranean rumble which did not hurt him in the slightest, but which no amount of hurrumphing and hawking and spitting into his handkerchief would remove. It was annoying, that was all. Vines, trying to tempt him into error, tossed the ball higher and slower. Without thinking, his body adjusting instinctively, White shuffled a quick pace down the wicket – one, one-two, like a ballerina – and bat met ball perfectly on the half-volley. It sped away past mid-off's left hand – a copy-book off-drive for four. The applause rippled round the ground – by now there was quite a number of spectators under the trees and spread along the boundary, as villagers finished the Sunday lunchtime washing-up and wandered down in the fickle sunshine. The swings in the far corner of the field, tarmacadamed for safety and convenience by the parish council, were in constant action, for this was the recreation ground as well as the cricket field – 'And don't you forget it, Mr Gauvinier,' as Mrs Verrall, the postmistress and chairman of the WI, once told him at a parish meeting.

White thought: 'There can't be much wrong with me if I can hit 'em like that,' suppressed a cough and turned the next ball neatly off his toes with a flick of the wrist, leaning into the shot and sauntering up the pitch for a single as he watched long leg wait for the ball to run straight into his hands some fifty yards from the batsman. Whether it was an uneven piece of ground, or a possible post-prandial misjudgement, long leg fumbled the ball. It hit his wrist, painfully, for it was still travelling fast, and ricocheted ten yards away to his right. 'Come on, two there,' yelled Trine, and banged his bat down at the crease, turning as he did so to run again. White, accelerating, made the second run just before the return came in, first bounce, to the keeper, and doubled over his bat, gasping for breath.

'Don't worry . . . I'll be okay . . .' He straightened up and waved away the solicitous fielders. He closed his mouth tightly and breathed deeply twice through his nose, filling his lungs, calming his thumping heart. That was better. It was the end of the over, too, and he leaned on his bat, to avoid any possibility of a fuss. Trine came up to him.

'Are you sure you're all right, Paul? You look white as a sheet.'

'Don't fuss, for Chrissake. It's nothing. Too many bloody fags, that's all. It'll go.'

'Don't you think you'd better go off?'

'Jesus Christ, leave me alone. I'm all right, I tell you.'

'If you say so.' Trine was still doubtful. 'We'll keep off the quick singles, anyway.'

'That's right.' White managed a grin. 'We'll get'm in fours.'

And Trine did contrive to hit two boundaries, a six and a four, in the next over, and off the last ball skied a massive catch almost perpendicularly double the height of the chestnut trees. Spicer at mid-on positioned himself under it nicely and held the catch and Trine, who'd run anyway in case the ball was dropped, continued without pause on his way to the pavilion, laughing and calling 'Well caught, John.' Spicer, genuinely pleased, called back 'Thought it was never coming down,' and jerked the ball hard back to Dewbury, taking the big black man by surprise and making him drop it. 'Come on, wake up, there, Constantine, you've got the real batsman in now,' as young Haynes, slim and looking younger than his fifteen years, with pads that were a size too large for him, made his way to the wicket.

Trine had hit thirty runs, and with White had added fifty for the sixth wicket in half an hour. With Tillingfold 127 for six, Gauvinier felt better. At least the village had avoided the embarrassment of a disastrous collapse before lunch, despite the hat-trick, and would give the President's XI a good run for their money. There was nothing worse than a gala day which petered out in mid-afternoon into a 'beer match' of ten overs a side, everyone bowling an over. In fact, Gauvinier only tolerated these in order to 'give a knock' to the lower-order batsmen, who sometimes hardly wielded a bat in earnest all the season when Tillingfold were on form.

Gauvinier went across to congratulate Trine, highly pleased with his knock and his three sixes and not at all put out by being caught off a skier.

'All right for you, Guv?' Trine inquired cheerfully. 'Scoreboard's looking a bit happier, I think. We could top 200 at this rate.' Trine was always optimistic. 'I'm a bit worried about young Paul, though.'

'Why, what's up? He seems to be batting very well. Timing it nicely.'

'We–ell, he's not feeling too good out there. Puffing and panting like a steam engine, and he's as white as chalk. I asked him if he wanted to come off for a spell and he more or less told me to piss off.'

'Great shot!' Gauvinier exclaimed. 'There's not much wrong with that.'

White, leaning back to give himself room, had cut Vines's top-spinner almost out of Dewbury's gloves, square of third man, for another four to take his score up to forty. 'Out of breath or not, that young man's batting like a master. Oh-oh.'

Vine's next ball, shorter and turning quite sharply, cut back very low off the pitch, and White, stabbing down on it, got an inside edge that flicked the ball away, narrowly missing the leg stump, and beat Dewbury's drive to his left as it sped to the deep field for two runs. 'Oh, dear.'

In the past half-hour the clouds had massed over the Downs and the sun had disappeared. Gauvinier had been watching the skyline with increasing apprehension, and when the clouds began to blur the outline of the Downs, he knew there was no hope. Now the wind freshened suddenly and the first scuds of rain swept across the pitch, causing the players to look up anxiously. The Union Jack, flying bravely at the flagpole atop the pavilion, stood out momentarily parallel to the roof and dropped listless again as the squall passed. 'I'm afraid we're in for it, Teddy,' said Gauvinier with the resignation of experience. 'Just when I was beginning to think of a declaration, too.'

He was right. Before the next over could begin, another, heavier shower sent the players scurrying for the pavilion, the bowlers seizing their sweaters from round the umpires' waists, tugging them over their heads as they ran. The batsmen followed more sedately, their legs suddenly weighed down by their pads. Gauvinier met White.

'Are you okay, Paul?'

'Fine now, Guv. It was just a turn. Bloody nuisance this rain. I could do with a fifty today.'

'Well, sit down and take the weight off your feet. Mind you, I don't think you'll have much chance for many more runs. It looks to have settled in for the day.'

Indeed the rain was sweeping across the darkened field in gusts, pattering on the windows and rattling the roof. A few spectators still huddled in the tents and under the chestnut trees in forlorn groups, but most had hurried to their cars or back to the village when the rain broke.

'That's a desolate scene, Peter. I don't think we'll see any more cricket today. What a damn shame.' Oliver Fanshawe sat with his umpire's coat-tails lifted on to the front of his thighs, like an old-fashioned frock-coat, and bent forward on his knees. 'It'll do the wicket good, anyway. Not that we need it, this year.'

Spicer pushed his way through.

'What d'you think, Peter? Any chance? One or two of my classier brethren want to call it a day.'

'Oh, not yet, John,' Gauvinier protested. 'Let's give it until four and then decide. You never can tell, with this changeable weather. And who's going to eat all the tea?'

'Not to worry about that. Not many of us want to pass up a

Tillingfold tea, you can be sure. It's just that my county youngsters have got to get back to Hove tonight. They're off first thing in the morning.'

The windows of the pavilion were beginning to steam up as the temperature of the outside air fell sharply with the rain. It smelt steamy and of male bodies. The studs of the boots crunched on the hard wooden floor.

'Boots off, everyone. Boots off,' called Fanshawe, authoritatively. Although the pavilion belonged to the parish council it was part of the lease that the cricket club kept it in good condition, and the wooden floor had seen much better days. Gauvinier grinned at him. 'You never give up, do you, Oliver?'

'Not if I can help it, Peter. Which reminds me—' he moved closer and spoke into Gauvinier's ear. 'How did you get on with the *Bugle* man?'

'Oh, quite well. He doesn't like Renton, though.'

'Join the club. But he's being quite useful.'

'That's what I told Weighall. He said to watch him.'

'We will. By the way, what's wrong with young White? I thought he was going to pass out, once or twice.'

'That's what Trine said when he came in just now. I'd better see if he's all right. I told him to have a rest.'

He looked around the crowded pavilion. Several players had already dragged chairs up to the trestle tables and had started a game of pontoon with a pack of cards produced by Jess. Others were sitting talking, or just standing, hands in pockets, staring at the rain. There was no sign of White. Gauvinier poked his head round the dressing-room door and saw the youngster stretched out on a locker, his eyes closed and his arms folded across his chest, heedless to the clatter around him. He was asleep. Gauvinier did not disturb him.

'He's having a kip,' he told Fanshawe. 'It'll do him good.'

He went to the little kitchen at the back of the pavilion and found Rosie Hunter, deep in conversation with Fred Bason. She looked flushed.

'Excuse me, Rosie, didn't want to disturb you, but do you

think we might have the tea a bit early today? We might as well get it over with, just in case the rain stops.'

'You can't have it before the urn boils, and you know how long that takes,' she said tartly.

'Oh, come on, Rosie. I know you can work wonders.' Coaxingly.

'Well,' she relented slightly. 'I did think you'd ask, so I put it on early. Half an hour do?'

'Fine, bless you, Rosie. I don't know what we'd do without you girls, do you, Fred?'

'Go on with you. You think a bit of flattery will get you anywhere. You're all the same, you men.'

'You know you love us.' He patted her on the arm and turned back into the pavilion. It was difficult to make himself heard over the din. The cigarette smoke was thickening, making him cough. He found a chair and jumped on it, one foot on the chair seat, the other on the table in the middle of the card game.

'Quiet please, everyone. Listen. We're going to have tea in half an hour, at four o'clock, and then make a decision about play. Everyone welcome, ladies as well, if you don't mind standing up. Now if you wouldn't mind clearing the trestles so Rosie and her girls can set tea, it won't be long.'

There was a muffled cheer, and a general shuffling as people moved back from the table. Gauvinier heard his name called.

'Guv! Guv! Over here. Guv!' It was Edward Trine, gesticulating at him from the dressing-room door. 'You'd better come here, quick. It's Paul. I can't make him speak. I – I think he's passed out or something.'

There was a sudden hush through the big room. Gauvinier thrust through the players. 'All right, all right. Don't panic. Stand back, don't crowd.' He thought he sounded like a policeman.

Paul White was lying in exactly the same position as when Gauvinier had seen him ten minutes before. He was not breathing.

Chapter 7

Alex Weighall's 'Sporticle' ('The Column No Sportsman Can Afford to Miss') in the *Daily Bugle* a few days later carried the whole story, headlined 'TEST MATCH AT TILLINGFOLD'. Weighall ('hard-hitting, analytical'), a discursive writer who liked to lead his readers into his subject by easy stages, began:

'Village cricket is more than a game. It is, to quote the late A. G. McDonnel, an art. And the match that I watched in not-so-sunny Sussex on Sunday had just about everything. There was a hat-trick. There were huge sixes. There was good batting and bad. True to form in this disastrous summer, Rain Stopped Play even before the home side could finish its innings. And to complete the illusion, nay, belief, that village cricket is a slice of life, we even had a near-fatality and a young man Saved by the Kiss of Life, administered in the best traditions by his Captain.

'It was all of no importance to any but the good villagers of Tillingfold . . . and yet, was that all? For the idyllic picture of white-flannelled figures on a green field, with the church spire rising behind the chestnut trees, is about to become a battleground on which will be fought issues of major importance not only to Tillingfold but to the whole of cricket and, indeed, possibly to the future of the English countryside itself . . . and within the team itself, that battle has already started . . .'

Gauvinier, studying the piece in the Dog and Duck over a pint of bitter with Oliver Fanshawe, tapped the page and grinned.

'Well, he's done us proud. It's a bit much, but it gives the right slant to the whole stupid business.'

'I'd have been happier if he'd not muddled MacDonnell up with de Selincourt and misspelt his name anyway,' said Fanshawe dryly. 'Still, I don't suppose most of the *Bugle*'s public would have been any the wiser if he'd got it right. I'm glad he gave you a pat on the back.'

'That's a load of cobbler's,' said Gauvinier flatly. 'I just happened to be there and knew what to do because I'm married to an SRN. Not that I want to repeat the process. Faugh!' He grimaced. Fanshawe smiled sympathetically.

'None too hygienic a proceeding, I gather.'

'I can think of more savoury contacts than stale curry, garlic and tobacco, thanks very much . . . and I gather that my intervention was probably quite unnecessary. He'd have come round anyway.'

'What was wrong with him?'

'I'm not sure. Some sort of aneurism. He's fine now. He'll be out of hospital in a couple of days, and he even had the nerve to ask me to keep a place for him this weekend. And where were his fags, if you please?'

Fanshawe laughed. 'Well, whatever they say about that young man he's got spirit. We could do with a few more like that. Have you seen the Colonel about calling the parish meeting?'

'Yes. He's got to give seven days' notice. That makes it next Wednesday at the earliest. He wanted to hold it early, at seven, but I persuaded him to make it at eight, to allow the commuters a chance to get there. Oh, and a piece of really good news. Lady Trine's volunteered the WI to take over the distribution of the appeal leaflets and petition forms, provided we get them printed.

I don't know what her good ladies are going to say, but the fair Elizabeth usually has her own way in these matters.'

He was right. Lady Elizabeth Trine, wife of Sir Edgar, had been Milady in her own right as Hon. Elizabeth Pryce-Walters, daughter of the Duke of Gwynneth. She had been an avant-garde of the twenties, a First at Girton with a bright future as a lawyer, historian, antiquary, novelist – the world was at her feet. She'd chucked it all to run a soup kitchen for the miners during the '26 strike, driving her bull-nosed Morris back to the family seat near Chepstow at the weekends for a bath and to ride to hounds. In the early thirties she'd disappeared for more than two years to nurse for Schweitzer at Lambarene, shipped back more or less by force when her health gave out due to repeated doses of malaria and dysentery. At thirty, she astounded society at large, and her family in particular, by making the one marriage nobody would ever have dreamed of for her. Old Lord Gwynneth had long since inured himself to the prospect of a coal miner or a naked black tribesman as a son-in-law, having given up hope of her marrying into her own class, as he preferred to call it. But you could have knocked him down with a feather when his daughter had calmly announced that she was marrying Lieutenant Edgar Trine, only son of a Sussex yeoman farmer, as dull a stick and as unlikely a mate for his meteoric daughter as he could have imagined. But when he tackled her about it, expressing his misgivings in the sing-song Welsh lilt he always adopted to hide his deeper feelings, she replied, simply, 'But I love him, father.' Her face, gaunt from her illness and surprisingly pale despite its exposure to the tropic sun, softened from within and Lord Gwynneth, watching her closely, was content. When he died towards the end of the war, worn out from working a twenty-hour day for five consecutive years without leave in an obscure ministry in Whitehall coping with Churchill's eccentricities, her share of his estate, after death duties, came to £300,000. Edgar, now leading his battalion through Normandy, was reading her letter sitting in the turret of his tank and hardly noticed the footnote, scrawled up the side of the writing on the last page

'. . . from your Loving Elizabeth. P.S. Don't worry about the stables. I'll see to them. Daddy left me three hundred gees.' He read it again, tilting back his steel helmet, working it out, recalling their own special code for their own special things, when a German sniper took aim and fired. Trine woke up to find his driver cradling him in his arms and blood, his own, covering them both. He had a dreadful headache. He put his hand up to discover a long wound neatly parting his hair and the skin of his skull.

Forty-eight hours later, the Battalion MO, catching up with the attack, insisted on examining him.

'Edgar, you bloody fool, you should be in hospital.'

'Why, for God's sake? I've only got a bit of a headache.'

'Well, you've had just about the luckiest escape you could have. You've been creased. A sixteenth of an inch lower and you'd have been dead.'

'— off! Ouch. What's that, brimstone?'

'Just hot water. What the hell d'you mean by sticking your head out of the top of a tank? You're not supposed to do that in the middle of an ambush. It's not in King's Regs.'

'I was reading a letter. Letter? Hey, doc, I've just remembered. I'm rich.'

'You won't be anything at all unless you lie down and stay still. Do you want to go home? This is a blighty one if ever I saw one.'

'Oh, Lord, no. There's nothing to spend it on now, anyway. I'll wait until after the war.'

And after the war he and Elizabeth used a healthy whack of the £300,000 in restoring and modernizing Tillingfold Hall; and Edgar retired from the army with a Military Cross when his time was up, even though he was offered a command. By virtue of his position in the village, his wealth and his family connections he was elected chairman of the parish council, and he progressed as a Conservative in turn to the old rural district council and thence to the county council, from which he retired after fifteen years' service, for which he received a knighthood. He affected tweed suits and a white moustache after the style of the comedian Jimmy Edwards, whom he resembled. Gauvinier, whose radical beliefs were regarded with suspicion by many of the older countrymen, and who suffered fools hardly, retained quite a large measure of respect for Colonel Sir Edgar Trine and a healthy wariness of Lady Trine. She played the squire's lady to perfection; and yet her manner always suggested that she was laughing at herself. A few years back, Fanshawe's researches had suggested that the club might be celebrating its 150th anniversary, so they decided to make an occasion of the President's match. The Trines (inevitably) provided a silver trophy for the winning team and little plaques for each player as a memento. They set out trestle tables in front of the pavilion and covered them with newly laundered white cloths. The evening sun winked off the shining silver, but the real dazzlement was provided by Lady Trine, now seventy, diamonds gleaming at her throat and wrists, her fingers encrusted with rings, her blonde head rivalling the sun. It was an incongruous scene but wholly pleasing, the players still in their white flannels holding their champagne glasses with the bubbles rising in the setting sun, slaking the thirst of a long afternoon in the field. The squire's speech, introducing his wife to present the cup, predictable as the tides but none the worse for that. And then Lady Trine, holding the trophy aloft, regally requesting an arm from Gauvinier. With two swift steps, she was standing on the table; as they looked on astounded, she began to sing. The deep contralto voice held them, falling over the quiet field:

'There'll always be an England, and England shall be free . . .' and they replied, almost as if they had been in church, with one voice:

'If England means as much to you as England means to me.'

Gauvinier often thought of that scene. His intellect told him it was schmaltz, embarrassing, sentimental rubbish. It wasn't. Elizabeth Trine stepped down from the table, fished a fly out of the champagne with a forefinger, knocked the full glass back in one and presented the cup as though nothing had happened at all. When he went to enlist her help he asked her why she had done it.

'I just felt like it,' she answered.

'Weren't you embarrassed?'

'Good heavens, no.' She laughed. 'Were you?'

'At the time I was not. But I remember being surprised at not being, if you see what I mean.'

'You were lucky it wasn't "Knees Up Mother Brown",' she said. 'It might quite easily have been.' He looked quizzical.

'Albert Schweitzer was the greatest man I ever knew,' she said calmly. 'Including Edgar over there, of course. And when he told me always to do precisely what I felt like doing, I believed him. "Elizabeth," he would say, "there's nothing in the world you can't do if you really put your mind to it." I wanted to sing, so I sang.'

'You could have been laughed at.'

'I wouldn't have heard it,' she replied. And he believed her.

'I need your help,' he said now, encouraged. Over seventy, she was as sharp as ever.

'I know. This Superstores thing. Edgar believes it will ruin the village. He may be right, he may not. "Ruin" is a relative term. When Edgar's father was the squire, only fifteen houses in the village had indoor toilets and only five had baths. There was no central heating and no sewage; and in the winter ten families had to share a bucket as a lavatory in a hut outside on the green. It was "progress" when Edgar's grandfather built the village school. Now it's "progress" again when the county council wants to close it down. Don't you sometimes think the world is turning upside down?'

'Oh yes. I often feel like Lord Peter Wimsey, hankering after an outmoded set of shibboleths. There's no sense in this scheme, just the logic of greed. But they can pay for the best advice, the top counsel, to prove to the world that they *must* do it. And afterwards, everyone says: "How could they allow it?" By "they" they mean the people who live in the place. That's us, and this time we've got to bring some sanity into the position before we all go mad.'

'Do you think the cricket club can do anything effective?'

He explained to her Weighall's theory of persuading cricketers throughout the country to bring their influence to bear. 'Create a climate of opinion,' he said, 'where it will be impossible for Superstores to move without offending someone high up. We are writing to every cricket club in the country, asking them to come in on our side. We won't ask for funds. Just for their support to shame Beeston out of his scheme to destroy 150 years of tradition to make another million for himself.'

'How can I help?'

'We need someone to organize the mailing. We're getting a letter out to around 10,000 cricket clubs asking for help – and signatures. We've written to the county secretaries already asking for names and addresses on their lists. When these come in we'll need envelopes addressed and sent out.'

'And you'll need money for postage, telephones, etc, etc.'

'That's right. We wondered if the WI and the other ladies' organizations might like to help us organize a collection or a raffle to raise money for postage and stationery and things.'

Lady Trine smiled. 'Well, we can always call for volunteers,' she said. 'I'll start things off. There's a meeting of the Institute tonight. I am sure we will find any number of helpers. There's nothing my ladies like better than a good cause, even though I don't suppose any of them will have played cricket.'

'Did you?' inquired Gauvinier.

'Young man, when I was younger that would have been regarded as an insolent remark. But for your information I was a left-arm fast bowler at Roedean.'

'Good God!' Gauvinier went away laughing. 'Thank God for organizing women,' he said to himself as he pedalled round to the vicarage to spread the word. He found Mrs Veyzey already in control; her Ladies' Circle was more active in the village than its parent body, the Billington and District Round Table, and already she had six letter-writers busy writing personal appeals to Rotary Clubs and Round Tables; and of course, Inner Wheels.

'What you need, Peter, is a really spectacular event. Something really big, that will catch people's imagination. What about a big cricket match?'

Gauvinier shook his head. 'I'd love to do something like that, but we couldn't lay it on until next year. If we can stall the issue for that long we might be able to get the county down for a special benefit game, or something like that. But it's too late for us. By that time the Superstores thing will be over and settled, one way or another.'

However, the idea of a big 'spectacular' stuck in his mind, and that evening he raised it at the meeting of the 'Save Tillingfold Committee', held round coffee and biscuits in his dining-room.

They thrashed the idea around for more than an hour, without success. The main objections to most of the proposals were expenses and the time needed to organize. Polly Gauvinier brought in a fresh supply of coffee and was struck by their obvious lack of enthusiasm.

'Why all the long faces?' she asked. 'Anything anyone can do?'

Albert Jess, who liked Polly, grinned up at her like a small demon from between the fingers thrust through his hair.

'You see the STFA, not the STC,' he said. 'This isn't the Save Tillingfold Committee. It's the Sit Thinking of Fanny Adams lot. If you can dream up a way in which we can bring this bloody Superstores development plan down in one fell swoop, then let us know. We've been cudgelling our so-called brains for an hour and the best we've come up with is a fête. It'll be the fourth fête in Tillingfold this summer and even this village's supply of second-hand clothes has run out by now.'

'I see what you mean. It *is* difficult, isn't it?' Polly sat on the table and hugged her knees. 'I've already sold Aunt Mavis's biscuit barrel twice and bought it once this summer. There's an awful feeling of *déja vu* even when the price tickets have been taken off the things.'

She gathered up the empty coffee mugs.

'Oh, well, I'll leave you to it. I've got better things to do on my evening off.' Gauvinier felt slightly guilty. He had promised to take her out for a meal this evening, but the meeting was making little progress. 'I've got the lovely telly to watch. It's that mad, fascinating March series.' She paused in the doorway and turned. 'I *am* a fool. That's it. Why don't you organize a march? On London? On Parliament? On Lord's, for God's sake? That *will* put you on the map.'

'I can see the headlines now,' Jess chimed in. 'Whites in Whitehall. Bureaucrats bowled out in Cricket Crisis.'

'Can you expect a couple of thousand elderly cricketers in flannels and wielding cricket bats to worry Superstores?' Gauvinier asked sceptically.

'I don't see why not. They'd certainly worry Lord's if they trampled over the wicket just before a Test match,' said Jess.

'Oh, no,' Fanshawe protested. 'You can't expect us to damage Lord's wicket. That would be heresy. We'd lose support, not gain it.'

'I was only joking. Don't look so shocked, Oliver.'

'No,' said Gauvinier sharply stopping the discussion in its tracks. 'No. We're on the wrong lines. We're expecting cricketers in Andover and Ashby de la Zouch to come to our help, but people aren't like that. If we're going to organize a march or anything else, it must be Tillingfold that does it. The team itself, without any help from anyone outside the village. If anyone wants to come along, that's fine. But it must be Tillingfold's show.'

He spoke with the conviction of one who has seen the light. The others looked at him, impressed.

'Where do we march to?' asked Jess curiously. 'Who will we see?'

'That's easy. We march to Lord's, to petition the MCC for help to save our cricket pitch. On the way, we collect signatures in all the towns and villages we pass. Then up to Lord's and the MCC.'

He watched their faces and went on talking to give them time to think.

'Look. When I was in Ireland a few years ago, some hoteliers in one of the Galway towns – Oughterard, I think – got together and bought some land on which they wanted to make a golf course to attract American tourists. Well, all of this land was virtually derelict – all stone and ancient broken-down walls and no soil depth. All the hotel owners were Irish, or Irish firms at any rate. But since Cromwell, in that part of the world the Irish have been sensitive about land, and although they'd got a better than fair price for it the peasants banded together into a Protection Society to stop the land being used for the filthy tourists – from whom they got their livelihood anyway. So a public inquiry was held, and the protesters lost. They didn't have a case on any grounds at all. The land wasn't even tillable. After a while, the hoteliers brought in a bulldozer to begin the clearing of the fairways. So what did the protesters do? They blew up the bulldozer.'

Through the laughter, Fanshawe asked: 'Did it work? Was the golf course built? And what's that got to do with this case?'

'No, of course it didn't work. But the point is that it's no good protesting if you don't do it in the right way. I think this march will work; and if it fails we can still do something else. Even blow up the bulldozers. Hands up who's for the march.'

The hesitant hands went up, one by one. Gauvinier and Jess were appointed as the executive sub-committee, with Renton attached for publicity, to find out how many members of the club would take part in all, or any of the march, and to seek support among other Tillingfold bodies. Fanshawe's task was to fix the route; and in one frenetic evening on the telephone he had laid on promises of support from at least ten clubs on the way to London; they would play ten-over challenge matches with as many clubs as possible en route for Lord's.

In the meantime, the extent of the problem was revealed at the parish meeting called by Colonel Trine, when the full planning application was revealed for the first time. Amid cries of

'Shame', 'Frame-up', 'Cheat' the Colonel read out the letter from the planning committee:

'We have the honour to inform you that advance notice of intention to file an application for Planning Permission to develop the site "A" on the attached plan, for the purpose of erecting a retail trading estate (tentatively to be called the Tillingfold Trading Centre) consisting of not fewer than six and not more than twelve large-area stores, with appropriate access, storage and parking facilities, has been received from Messrs Handsome and Wellbeloved, of Down Street, Tillingfold. In conformity with the statute we would further inform you that certain discussions have already taken place with reference to the processing of this application, and it is the intention to hold a public inquiry at which any objections may be raised by private or public bodies or individuals. The inquiry will be conducted by Brigadier Alexander Smyth, DSO, County Councillor, and although a date and venue have not yet been finalized, it is hoped that the inquiry may be completed by the end of the third quarter of this year. Written objections may be forwarded to Brigadier Smyth at the County Council offices at any time; and any body or person who wishes to make any verbal representation to the Inquiry should notify intention of doing so before August 31.'

'. . . and I can tell you little more than that, ladies and gentlemen,' Colonel Trine told a meeting of more than two hundred packed into the village hall. 'The powers that be have obviously gone some way along the road to approving this application, or it would not have reached this stage already. My information is that there is not much we can do now except to object if we wish to the timing of the public hearing or to the person who has been appointed to look into the matter. If I may say so, I have known Brigadier Smyth for many years both in and out of the Army, and I have no hesitation in recommending him to you as an impartial person of the highest integrity.'

Colonel Trine paused. 'On the other hand, it could be that some of you may think that the village would be better off in the hands of a detached official from Whitehall – a faceless civil servant with no axe to grind. We on the Parish Committee know that you will wish for us to take a lead in these matters, and our recommendation is that we should do three things:

'One: to notify the planning committee of Tillingfold Parish Council's intention to object to this plan on the grounds that (a) it will destroy the character of the village as it has been known for hundreds of years and (b) that it will create disastrous problems for miles around through countryside much of which is designated as an area of natural beauty.

'Two: to request a deferment of the date of inquiry to give the parish more time adequately to prepare its case; and Three: to confirm that we are satisfied with the appointment of Brigadier Smyth to chair the inquiry, but ask for two Ministry Assessors to sit with him.'

He sat down to muted applause. The broad sunburnt Sussex faces stared at him earnestly. You could never tell with these people, he thought. Once he would have said that he knew them, knew which way they would jump. And yet now it wasn't so certain. Perhaps it was because modern means of communications had brought the world closer to Tillingfold, and with it different people, new standards. Like the bland-faced Mitterman, who was rising smoothly to his feet.

'May I have a word, Mr Chairman?' Every head turned, silently. There was no impoliteness, yet Trine felt the hostility rise like a solid wall. Mitterman showed no sign of unease.

'Mr Chairman, may I say at once that I represent some of the interested parties in this scheme, and that, quite by coincidence, I am also a resident of this village. My wife and I have lived here for the past five years.'

There was a murmur. It rippled across the hall from one side to the other and died. Mitterman continued in his high, pedantic voice.

'I am authorized to say that in making this application, my colleagues have been concerned to cause as little disruption of Tillingfold life as possible.' He held up his hand to quieten the louder rumble of disbelief. '. . . indeed, apart from the benefit of at least 500 more jobs which will be created in the area, there will be the increased benefit of first-class roads. It has long been true that Tillingfold has been cut off from the mainstream of the life of the rest of the country by poor communications. This development will place Tillingfold squarely astride a new roadway linking the major motorways to the south coast, giving ease of accessibility, the lack of which has hampered the progress of Tillingfold for many years in the past.'

The murmurs had been growing from generalized distrust to open dissent. Calls of 'We don't want your progress' and 'What's in it for you?' and 'What about the cricket club?' began to drown Mitterman's smooth exposition. A slight flush mounted high on his cheekbones.

'As far as the cricket club is concerned, it is our intention that it will not be harmed in any way. Rather, we shall acquire a new suitable field, have it levelled professionally and a new square laid. We are prepared to grant the club an interest-free loan for twenty years to build a new pavilion.' He paused, leaned forward with both hands on the back of the chair in front of him, and looked round earnestly at the audience. They stared back, red-faced and stolid. There was some shuffling of feet and re-crossing of legs.

'Ladies and gentlemen, we are well aware that there will be opposition – genuine opposition – from those who feel that Tillingfold should be preserved as it were in aspic forever. I ask you, look around. No one could call the village historic, in any sense of the word. There is no great church, or great county seat, to give it an elegant identity. At best the village architecture is a result of a combination of apathy and arrogance of the speculators of the past. There is not one Scheduled Building in the entire neighbourhood of adequate quality to be preserved for posterity. It is time Tillingfold ceased being a non-place and entered the twentieth century.'

There was more rumbling with a few ragged 'hear hears'.

'As much as I respect the wishes of the chairman, I must point out that in this matter time, as always, waits for no man. The pressure of modern developments is rapid, and my colleagues wish to proceed as speedily as possible towards the finalization of their plans. Therefore, I would move a counter-motion that the inquiry proceed as rapidly as possible; it is in the interests of every one of us here that the whole matter should be aired completely, but there is no need for delay. It is no use beating about the bush.' He glanced around the cramped room, the bare plaster walls, the wooden chairs, many the worse for wear. 'To begin with, the village could do with a new hall for public meetings.'

There was another rumble as Frank Hunter, red-faced, pushed himself to his feet to second Mitterman's motion. Gauvinier, too, was standing, trying to catch the chairman's eye and to make himself heard above the increasing din.

'There's summat in what the man says . . .'

'No point in hangin' about . . .'

''Tain't much of a village really, now, ennit?'

'Bloody cricket club . . . load of snobs anyway, there . . .'

'Five hundred jobs, he said . . .'

'Hunter's in on it, and Bason too, you'll see. Wonder who else will get a cut? . . .'

'Mr Chairman . . . Mr Chairman . . .'

Colonel Sir Edgar Trine thumped his fist down on the table, for lack of a gavel.

'Quiet everybody. Q–U–I–E–T! Silence for Mr Gauvinier.'

The Colonel's voice was formidable, and within a few seconds Gauvinier was able to speak comfortably. The pause had given him time to think.

'Mr Chairman, I want to support the motion from the chair calling for a full and proper inquiry into this scheme, but before I speak to this, may I have your permission to put two or three questions to my friend Mitterman?'

Sir Edgar looked inquiringly at Mitterman, who nodded his head and rose to his feet. He was on the opposite side of the room from Gauvinier, and the villagers followed the exchange with close attention, their heads moving from side to side as the exchanges proceeded, like the spectators at the Centre Court at Wimbledon.

'Mr Mitterman; are you able to say how many of these large stores are planned for the Tillingfold site; and how many of these are subject to firm offers?'

'The Tillingfold Centre is planned for a minimum of seven, maximum of twelve stores, with appropriate car parking. I am not authorized to say how many firm offers have been taken up so far. The scheme is only at planning stage.'

'I see. And what is the total value of the project?'

'At current estimates, about thirty million pounds.'

'Of which your commission would be, say ten per cent?'

There was a gasp. The village was accustomed to rich residents; but it did not often rub shoulders with anyone who made a cool three millions on one deal. Mitterman answered stiffly:

'I am unable to give any personal details of that nature.'

'Thank you, James, that's all I have to ask at this stage.'

Gauvinier turned to the chairman. 'Sir Edgar, in seconding the motion from the chair, I would like to say only this at this juncture. My friend James Mitterman there may have three million good reasons—' (laughter) '—good reasons why he wishes to bulldoze this scheme through without adequate time for discussion or examination of what it really entails. I believe, and I know there are many like me, that any such scheme will be not only disastrous but totally destructive of Tillingfold as we know it.' ('Hear, hear.') 'Believing this, a number of villagers have set up the Save Tillingfold Committee to fight to prevent its ever coming into being. As you may know, the Women's Institute and the Ladies' Circle are already hard at work. Lady Trine, Mrs Veyzey and Miss Millington at the Post Office have petition forms and if anybody has any bright ideas I'd be grateful if they'd let me know.

'However, the main thing is to know what we're up against, and this meeting is the first time any of us have had any real knowledge of what is planned for the village. I for one am not sure that we've heard it all yet.'

He paused. He did not want to say too much. It was all too easy, he knew, to be carried away by a sympathetic audience.

'I just want to say this. Life in Tillingfold has always been pretty good, in spite of everything. It's not so much a question of burying our heads in the sand, but here tucked in behind the Downs we've been protected from most of the rough winds of the twentieth century. I want it to stay that way. We've missed the railway, and the motorway, and the airport, and the new town. I reckon we can go on doing without them for a few hundred years more . . . All we want to do is to preserve Tillingfold's way of life, and we don't want to have to do a UDI to do it.'

Gauvinier sat down amid a storm of clapping, and the parish council's motion was passed by a substantial margin on a show of hands.

'So far so good,' he told Renton as they strolled down with Fanshawe to the Dog and Duck after the meeting. Renton was rubbing his hands over another good story, but Fanshawe was not yet convinced that the village vote was enough.

'You know, there were at least thirty hands in favour of Mitterman. It could multiply later.'

'Indeed it could,' said Gauvinier heavily.

Chapter 8

Gauvinier woke up the following morning to a dream of trumpets calling him to battle and to the sound of a letter falling with a gentle thump on to the front door mat. Polly brought it to him with a hot cup of tea and a cool kiss. The red bugle in the top left-hand corner of the envelope reminded him of his dream, and set him to wondering idly at extra-sensory perception and if it worked during sleep. Springing from the mouth of the little instrument were the words ' We Trumpet the Truth.' Inside was a cheque for £25 made out to Tillingfold Cricket Club and a note from Weighall.

'Enclosed is a small donation from the *Bugle* for services rendered. I thought you'd prefer it made out to the club rather than to yourself. I hope you liked my piece.

'Two suggestions.

'1. Extract from Renton on pain of death or excommunication the information he gleaned at Tyling Manor the other night. If not Renton, Trine Junior may know something, although I doubt it.

'2. If you want to tackle Beeston direct, it might be helpful to know that he too plays cricket (not well) for Ashley-on-Thames, a small exclusive club near Henley.

'Good Hunting.'

Mystified, he showed it to Polly. She could make as little of it as he could. All was explained when he saw Renton later the same morning in the Dog and Duck. Renton passed over a single sheet of copy paper.

'That's the story I'm going to put in tomorrow's *Bugle*,' he told Gauvinier. 'Gossip column. That's why it's written like that. Sorry.'

Gauvinier saw at once what he meant. The short article was written in the unctuous style of the gossip-columnist: the name-drop, the stale news and the innuendo combining to serve up the accustomed brew.

'The subject of that delicious tit-bit (no pun intended) which so intrigued thousands at this year's Royal Academy exhibition, I can now reveal exclusively, is none other than Mrs Winifred Mitterman, the wife of one James Mitterman, a familiar figure in lofty but obscure parts of the City.

'Aha, you may cry, but *who* is she? No less than the third daughter of the Earl of St Leonard's, whose coming-out ball, *Bugle* readers will recall, became just that when the ladies arrived topless and the gentlemen, dare it be said, came bottomless. And they all ended up motherless.

'This fascinating lady was recently seen, in company with her husband, kicking the light fantastic and *very* scantily dressed, with tycoon Sir Philip Beeston, no less, and his latest secretary, the aptly named Hon. Pauline Wilder, and certain local worthies at an hostelry not a million miles from the village of Tillingfold, subject of the acquisitive Sir Philip's latest multi-million pound venture.

'Could Sir Philip be said to be talent-spotting? And we don't mean on the local cricket pitch.'

'Spicy,' Gauvinier told Renton. 'But it's not all that new. Most of the village has known about that dinner party for the past two weeks. That's not going to do us a bit of use, fine though it might be for you.'

Renton, stung, leaned forward across the table and tapped Gauvinier on the chest. Gauvinier shrugged him off irritably. He hated to be touched. Renton paid no attention. He whispered, fiercely:

'I know that. That's not important. What is important is what I can't print. Nor can Weighall or the *Bugle*. There's no proof. But you see where it says "certain local worthies"?'

Gauvinier nodded.

'I'm certain that one of them was Brigadier Smyth, the county planning man. The same bloke who's going to chair this inquiry.'

'Well, so what? There's nothing wrong in Smyth having dinner with Beeston or anyone else for that matter.'

'Maybe not, but your young Smith's got a girl friend who works at the Manor as a waitress. She's Arabella something-or-other. She knows about the dinner because she waited at table. Young Trine was there too, and he got fresh – put his hand up her skirt, so she dropped his dinner down his front. The manager, who's a pal of Trine's, wanted to sack her but to give him his due, Trine said it was all his fault, which it was. The point is, Arabella's got a sister, Araminta, and she persuaded Thompson, the banqueting manager, to take 'Minta on as a hat-check girl for the evening.'

Renton paused, spread his hands and opened his eyes wide. It was a perfect caricature of an outraged young miss. Gauvinier laughed in spite of himself.

'I saw 'Minta, and she told me this. Apparently Smyth – or the one she and Thompson think is Smyth – didn't go to the dinner, but came along later and joined them for coffee. He and Beeston and Mitterman – she knows Beeston because she heard him called Sir Philip – went to the loo for a private chat. They had to pass through the hat-check place and asked 'Minta to keep an eye out and not let anyone in while they were talking.

'After a bit Mitterman and Beeston came out alone, chatting. She heard Beeston say: "Cheap at half the price," and Mitterman hushed him up. A bit later Smyth came out of the gents trying to hide a large envelope under his jacket. He asked for his brief-case, which she'd checked in, and put the envelope away and locked the case.'

'Interesting,' said Gauvinier, intrigued by the story. 'But how interesting? We don't know what was in the envelope.'

'Oh, there's more yet.' Renton grew even more confidential. Gauvinier thought the whole bar could hear his stage whisper. ''Minta's a smart girl and she can read upside down. Smyth's brief-case is one of those posh ones with two number locks – you dial the correct number to open the case and when you close it you just give it a twirl to lock it. Saves you losing the keys and in any case only you know the combination.'

Gauvinier nodded.

'Well, when he unlocked it to put the envelope in, 'Minta memorized the code. Then he told her to keep a special eye on it and went back into the restaurant to finish his drink, and 'Minta thought she'd take a peek. That envelope held around £500 – in used notes.'

Gauvinier stared in disbelief.

'How the hell do you know all this? And what does it mean?'

Renton grinned. 'It cost you three double gins and a tenner in cash. It'll be on my account. But at a push 'Minta would swear to it. She's nosey, not dishonest. And she'll make a good witness if necessary.'

'Did you tell Weighall this?'

'Yes, but he can't use it. It'd be libel. Nor can the *Bugle*, even in the smut column. In any case, there's only a suspicion. There's nothing in law that says a man can't carry around a brief-case full of notes, even if he is a county councillor. Frankly, I don't see how you can use it, even if it is true. The greater the truth, the greater the libel, we always say. And if you write to anyone, you'll be committing the libel yourself.'

'When's that appearing in the paper?' Gauvinier gestured to the written copy.

'Tomorrow or Saturday. When they've got room. I thought you ought to see it first.'

'Thanks. Oh, and let's keep this other thing quiet. It's useful to have up our sleeves anyway.'

'Don't worry. I'm used to keeping my sources quiet, and 'Minta won't talk. I told her she'd get twenty years if she so much as breathed a word. What are you going to do?'

Gauvinier had no intention of telling Renton of his plans, or of the tip-off he had received from Weighall. He dodged the question and went to find Fanshawe. As the result of their deliberations, for the first time he or anyone else could remember, Gauvinier stepped down from Tillingfold's Saturday match and Fanshawe regretfully withdrew from his customary task as umpire. They told no one their intentions; but not long after breakfast on the Saturday Oliver Fanshawe's three-wheeler set off boldly along the Sussex lanes, heading north for the Thames Valley.

'It'll be quite a change, just watching a match,' Gauvinier told Fanshawe, gritting his teeth and grasping the door handle as the little car sped along the narrow roads. They stopped in Twyford for a pub lunch and a little after one o'clock pulled off the road under a big willow tree at the lovely little cricket ground of Ashley-on-Thames. A wooden pavilion which might be categorized as 'quaint' presented a beamed and eaved double front to the ground, with matching scorebox like a doll's house alongside. Behind the pavilion the Thames ran, blue and tranquil beneath the clear sky, separated from the cricket field by newly painted white railings and a gravel towpath. They stepped gingerly on to the outfield, close-cropped and springy.

'How the other half lives.' Gauvinier was delighted. 'Look at this grass. Just like a bowling green. We could pitch Tillingfold's wicket at square leg here and we'd still think it was a beauty.'

Out in the middle the mown pitch lay ready for the afternoon's match, smooth enough to put many a county wicket to shame. The stumps looked as though they had just been removed from their plastic covers, erect, golden, symmetrical, the bails asleep exactly in their little grooves. With some satisfaction, Fanshawe pointed out that this was not correct; by custom and practice the umpires took the bails out with them at the start of play and removed them when they came off the field. The boundary was marked, a perfect oval, by little triangular flags in white linen, and the area around the pavilion was demarcated by a miniature picket fence, also in pristine white. A formidable notice, 'Members Only', adorned the entrance.

Slowly the teams assembled, stepping from a collection of Rolls-Royces, Jaguars and BMW's that would have graced a garage in Berkeley Square. The players were either middle-aged or very young. They had two things in common: the immaculacy of their flannels and their Oxford accents. Their ladyfolk draped themselves in brightly coloured deck-chairs whose stripes contrasted strongly with the muted pastel shades of the dresses, although here and there a pair of expensive slacks acknowledged the twentieth century. Presently the two captains, one in an all-green blazer ('Zingari?' inquired Gauvinier of Fanshawe *sotto voce.* 'No, Greenjackets,' came the hissed reply), the other in an MCC sweater and cap, made their solemn way to the wicket, and, after suitably grave inspection, MCC sweater produced a coin from a capacious trouser pocket and tossed it high. On the wind came a small cry of 'tails' and then the two skippers walked in together, MCC making bowling signs to his eager minions and Green Jacket calling: 'Put your pads on, Mike. And you John. Number three, Archie, if you don't mind . . .'

Gauvinier, feeling like a trespasser, invaded the 'Members Only' enclosure and braved the forbidding eyes of two matrons and a small girl in pink, with golden ringlets, and opened the door of the scorebox. Inside a small boy, looking uncommonly like Bobby Bewers, even though, unlike Bobby, he wore the well-scrubbed look of the prep school on parade, looked up and said, politely: 'Can I help you, sir?'

Gauvinier, blinking, asked if he might see the batting order; and discovered that the home side was fielding and the visitors, the Greenjackets indeed, were batting.

'Can you tell me, is Beeston playing?'

A pair of young eyes looked at him shrewdly.

'We've nobody of that name playing for Ashley, sir.'

'That's most odd. I understood Sir Philip Beeston played for you. Do you always score for them?'

'Only when I'm home from school and in the hols, sir. They pay me a pound a game, sir, and it helps out when I'm short, sir.'

Gauvinier became conscious of a very direct pair of schoolboy eyes looking at him. The emphasis on the penultimate word hit him.

'Well now, it is a bit difficult during the summer, isn't it, young man?' He put his hand in his pocket. 'What is your name?'

'Beeston, sir.'

Gauvinier looked at him and laughed out loud.

'For God's sake . . .'

The boy Beeston turned the page of the scorebook without speaking. His pencil ran down the list of batsmen in the previous week's game, as if it was seeking one particular name. Gauvinier silently slipped a 50p piece on to the page. It vanished without any noticeable movement and the pencil point hovered and then descended on number seven : B. Philip c and b Haverford, 23.

'My father keeps me *very* short, sir. He says it's good for my character. Thank you very much, sir.' Gauvinier slipped another 50p piece on to the scorebook. The schoolboy eyes looked at him with bland innocence.

'Does Sir Philip make many good scores?' asked Gauvinier.

'He gets mad when he doesn't. He's usually mad. But he's not a bad bowler. He's taken four wickets twice this season.'

'I'd like to talk to him. Do you think it would be better to approach him before or after the game?'

'If you're Press, never.'

Gauvinier shook his head vigorously. 'Nothing like that. A personal matter.'

'It's no use if you want to borrow any money. He's not that sort of man.' Gauvinier shook his head again.

'Blackmail?' The dark eyes shone.

'Sort of.' Gauvinier sensed an ally.

'Then it'll cost you another pound to stop me telling him,' said the boy Beeston calmly.

'Why don't you like your father, young man?'

'That is immaterial, sir. For one pound I will keep my counsel about your intentions. For two I will introduce you to him myself.'

He pocketed Gauvinier's pound notes. 'After the match.'

'How do I know you'll keep your word, young Beeston?' Gauvinier asked with some curiosity.

'You don't. Now, sir, if you wouldn't mind, I have to concentrate on scoring. The match is starting.'

Gauvinier paused. 'Where is your – Sir Philip fielding?'

'Silly mid-off, sir. It is a remarkably appropriate position.'

Gauvinier made his way back to Fanshawe. 'I've revised my opinion of young Bobby Bewers,' he said. 'Compared with that young gangster in there, Bobby is a small saint.'

'A product of the public school system, Peter?'

'If that's typical, it's no wonder we're going all comprehensive.'

He explained what had happened; and they settled down to watch an afternoon's cricket. To his surprise, they thoroughly enjoyed themselves. For all the smart caps and smarter accents, they came to the conclusion that Tillingfold's standards, if anything, were better than Ashley's, and the Greenjackets were a surprising mixture of the sublime and the gorblimey, as Gauvinier put it. The Greenjackets' fortunes rested on the prowess of two batsmen, who put on 140 together before being parted. At which the hot and sweating Ashley bowlers promptly took the next nine wickets for forty runs, and the Greenjackets innings closed just before tea on 183. 'Sir Philip' took three wickets with steady medium pacers, and also fielded well in his incongruous position, his body bent forward in a vulpine stance, his predatory eyes never leaving the batsman's face and his hands hooked like claws. There was no doubt he took his cricket seriously and also no doubt that he was a self-made player and not a 'natural'. Grim purpose showed through his every move. He batted stiffly for fifteen runs, at home to the quicker bowlers but hopelessly at sea, like so many club players, to the slower ball tossed up in the air and seemingly inviting to be hit. Gauvinier felt respect grow for the man, if not liking. Such intensity of purpose could well explain Beeston's progress from Huddersfield foundrymaster's son to tycoon. It wouldn't make him any easier to deal with. He wondered how to approach the whole subject and what sort of a hearing he would get. His problem was at least partially solved by the boy Beeston, who strolled languidly across to the little three-wheeler after Ashley had won the game by two wickets.

'My father asks you to excuse him. He never does business at the weekends,' said the self-possessed young man. 'He has asked me to deal with the matter. I've told him what it was.'

Gauvinier was annoyed.

'How d'you mean?' he demanded. He didn't recall telling this remarkable child anything – even his name. 'What exactly did you tell him?'

'I said that Mr Gauvinier from Tillingfold had come to try to talk him out of the Tillingfold project and wouldn't take no for an answer. I also advised him to listen to you. I said you hadn't come all this way unless you had something important to say.'

'How do you know who I am?'

'Oh, we saw you last Sunday, playing cricket. We parked under the chestnut trees. I think you'll be all right.'

'How on earth can you say that?'

'Oh, father always asks my advice, and he usually does what I tell him,' said the remarkable boy calmly. 'I have already calculated that his Tillingfold project will cost him six times his estimate and will lose him five million pounds in the first three years. Who wants Tillingfold? Stinking little hole,' he added scornfully in more juvenile idiom.

Seated beside Gauvinier, Fanshawe began to splutter. 'This is preposterous.' Gauvinier hushed him with both hands raised, patting the air in a series of hasty movements.

'I'm glad to hear it,' he said politely to the boy Beeston. 'You seem to be on my side. Why? If it isn't a rude question.'

'Not at all. I am fourteen. My father is fifty-four. With his blood pressure, his heart-rate, and his habits, his life expectancy is put at six years at the outside. I shall inherit his fortune before I am twenty. I have no intention of taking over a bankrupt empire. I see you find it difficult to believe me. Perhaps it will help to know that I have an IQ of 230-plus.' He spoke matter-of-factly. Slightly bemused, Gauvinier asked: 'Why the money? What was all that about?'

'The three pounds? I told you my father keeps me very short. I needed it to put down on a horse in the four-thirty at Sandown.'

Gauvinier stared. 'Oh come off it. This is too much.'

'It is quite true. Sticky Wicket. It came in at twenty-five to one.' He rifled through a wad of grubby banknotes. 'It belongs to my father. It was time it won. It's been held back for the last four races. I must go and get father. He relies on me to extricate him from the bar. Goodnight.'

He extended a cool hand, and was gone.

That evening, in the cool of his study, Gauvinier wrote a long letter to the Chief Constable.

Chapter 9

Gauvinier woke to the muted tinkle of his front doorbell, followed immediately, it seemed, by two loud knocks on the door. The sun was streaming in through the open window, but a bleary glance at his watch showed that it was only 6.30. He rolled out of bed reluctantly, grabbed his dressing-gown and slung it round his shoulders as he stumbled downstairs and almost unconsciously opened the door. The bright sunlight struck across his eyes and he stood blinking, for a moment or two unable to see anything at all.

'Sorry to wake you, Guv.' It was Steve Wally, the postman. 'Can't get 'em all through your letterbox.' Gauvinier stared at him. He was carrying a packet of letters of assorted sizes, held together by two thick rubber bands; there was a similar package under the other arm.

'Good God! Are they all for me?'

'Oh, yes, sir. And the postmaster asked me to ask you whether it was all right if he sends a van straight through from Billington later today with the rest.'

'The rest?' Gauvinier could hardly comprehend what the postman was saying.

'Oh, yes, sir. Don't worry, you'll wake up soon.' He thrust the second packet, heavier than the first, into Gauvinier's hands, and strode off to his bicycle, whistling.

'You must be popular,' he called back cheerfully. 'What 'ave you done? Won the pools?'

Gauvinier laughed, waking up. 'Not really,' he called back. 'It just feels like it.'

He hurried in to the kitchen, packets under his arm, picking up the *Telegraph* from the doormat. Rhodesia, economic policy and the TUC made familiarly depressing headlines. A smaller headline caught his eyes down the page. 'Former Pop Star Joins Cricket Club Crusade,' and he read how Albert Jess had given a short interview on the need to preserve Tillingfold CC.

Automatically he selected the smaller of the two teapots; found the caddy, and methodically emptied three teaspoonsful of Earl Grey into the pot. One each, one for the pot. As the kettle heated up, he found a table knife, and thrust it under the top envelope. He saw it was addressed to P. Gavinuer, Captain of Tillingfold, Sussex, in an untutored hand. The letter, on cheap lined paper, was to the point.

> Dere Mr Gavinnuer, I am 11 and I live in Sussex and I think the guverments roten to let yr cricket pich be plowed up. Keep it up.
>
> Love,
>
> Peter Pring
>
> PS My name's Peter two.

The second envelope bore a date stamp from Maltby, in Yorkshire. It was typewritten, and his name was correctly spelt. There was green letter-heading on the enclosure: 'South Maltby Cricket Club'. It read.

> Dear Skipper, I am instructed to convey to you the sympathy and support of the South Maltby Cricket Club and to

wish Tillingfold well in your fight to save your ground.

Happen you may need a hand later on. Count on us.

Yours sincerely,

Joe Everleigh

Secretary

Stapled to the letter was a cheque for £10. He looked at it in amazement, and then placed it carefully on the table. He called up the stairs.

'Come down here, Polly, love, and give us a hand. It looks as if we've got a job on.'

With Polly's help, and between bites of egg and bacon, it took them over an hour to open and peruse all the letters. They were mostly on the same lines, and twelve of them contained money; the largest amount a cheque for £25 from a retired general, and the smallest a postal order for 25p from another small boy. There was £53.75 in all.

'Thank the Lord for the vicar's wife and Lady Elizabeth,' said Polly, practically, looking at the pile. There were just over a hundred letters altogether. 'Now as well as sending out letters they'll be able to answer this lot and add up the cash. At least you'll be able to afford the awful Renton and his expense accounts.'

'Goodness knows what we do with it.' Gauvinier was worried. 'We're not a registered charity and we haven't appealed for cash, but it seems almost like taking money by false pretences.'

'Don't be so daft. Surely if that's the way people want to help you these days, they can do so. It may not be much, but it's at least useful.'

'It's certainly very encouraging. Except for that lot.' He picked up a missive in a plain brown envelope. There were four or five on its pile. He read out loud.

'Dear Tillingfold C.C., Your lot always squeals when its hurt. Well, you're hurt and you'll be bloody well more hurt when we've finished with you.'

It was unsigned, but the postmark was local. So was that on another from the same little pile. Gauvinier thought he could almost put a name to it.

'What about the rest of the bloody village? Don't you like being dragged into the 20th Century, with all your airs and graces? Give someone else a chance.'

Polly grimaced.

'It wouldn't be too hard to work out who sent that one,' she observed.

'You're taking the words out of my mouth,' he agreed. 'But I'm not going to try. D'you realize what this means?' With growing excitement. 'We're really going to be able to fight Beeston and his crowd now. Let's go and——'

She laughed. 'You really are a big kid. You know you'll have to get on with it yourself. I'm on duty at the hospital at ten and they can't spare me. We're ten nurses short of establishment already.'

'All right, all right,' grumbled Gauvinier. And, despite her pleas that eight o'clock in the morning was too early to visit people, he set off at a brisk trot to the Hall, where he was cordially invited to join the Trine family at their breakfast. Declining a second helping of bacon and eggs, Gauvinier accepted coffee and gave Lady Elizabeth and her husband a succinct resumé of his morning's mail.

'. . . and Steve – the postman, you know – said there was a stack more they're sending over by van. D'you think your ladies can rally round to help? I'll never be able to answer the lot. And someone's got to deal with the money . . .'

The Lady Elizabeth beamed at him.

'We're going to need a headquarters,' she said practically. 'I'd say you could use this house, but the Axminster's wearing a bit thin and I'm too old to be bothered with a lot of women clucking around and turning the place into a hencoop. Why don't you use the cricket pavilion? It's got the long tables, and it's summer time so it won't be too chilly. Anyway, you can always put in a couple of oil stoves. I'll give Stella Verrall a ring.'

She got up from the table, pressed a bell in the wall for the *au pair* girl to remove the breakfast things, and went out into the hall. Colonel Trine grinned at Gauvinier, tossed over a packet of cigarettes, and lit a large pipe for himself amid a cloud of fragrant blue smoke. Gauvinier wished for the umpteenth time that he had been able to manage a pipe. Colonel Trine gestured with the stem of his pipe towards the hall, whence his wife's voice could be heard, muffled by the distance into incomprehensibility. Soon there was a muted 'ting', and she returned, beaming.

'Stella was waiting for a call from you,' she said to Gauvinier. 'At a rough count you've got two thousand letters to get through from the first post, and there are five more sacks at the Billington sorting centre. Stella thinks she can get three of her WI members to start things off after lunch today if you can fix up the pavilion. What d'you want them to do?'

'Well,' began Gauvinier somewhat vaguely. 'I haven't really worked it out yet——'

She interrupted him briskly.

'Well, to start with you're going to need typewriters and some tables to put them on. You'll need a Gestetner or some sort of duplicating machine, probably an addressograph and certainly a whole lot of stationery. You've *got* to have someone dealing with the money and somebody else to dictate the answers and sort out the letters. You'd better do that, as you're the only one who'll be there who knows anything about what's going on. We don't want that nasty little Renton man trying to run things.'

'I can't understand why this thing's getting so big.' Gauvinier was still trying to work things out. 'All this can't have come from the one article, can it?'

'Why not?' she retorted. 'The *Bugle* claims to sell five million copies——' She was interrupted again by the telephone.

'Tillingfold six double five . . . hullo . . .?' She paused and then handed the instrument to Gauvinier. 'It's for you. Stella Verrall at the Post Office told them you were here – it's the BBC.'

Still bemused, Gauvinier found himself agreeing to be interviewed for Nationwide later the same day; hardly had he put the telephone down when it rang again. This time it was Southern TV on the same trail, with some additional requests.

'When's your next match, Mr Gauvinier?'

'Next Saturday, against Billington Seconds.'

'At home?'

'Yes, indeed. Two-thirty start.'

'We'd like to come and film the match – as part of a whole piece we'll be doing on Tillingfold and the scheme.'

'You're welcome.'

'By the way, has there been any response yet to the newspaper articles?'

'So far, it looks as though we've got about five thousand replies. Yes, we're setting up an appeal centre in the Pavilion. You'd like to come along today? Well, leave it until after three o'clock. All right, see you then.'

Gauvinier cradled the earpiece gently. He turned to Sir Edgar and Lady Trine, slightly flustered.

'I'd better get home. There's this lot of letters to answer, and God knows how many to come. I've got to be interviewed twice by TV and if it goes on like this, I don't know how I'm going to cope.'

Lady Elizabeth had experienced her fair share of the limelight in a varied life.

'You'll be surprised how much you'll enjoy the next few days, Peter,' she told him. 'You may not think you like the idea, or even want it, but when it's all over you won't want it to stop.'

Gauvinier laughed doubtfully, but her words turned out to be not too far from the truth. By that afternoon the postmistress had organized an efficient campaign office in the pavilion. Frank Hunter brought across one of the long banks of lights from his service bay and rigged it up across the centre of the pavilion, extra tables and chairs had been carried down from the village hall, and a complicated duplicating machine borrowed from the local office of the National Farmers Union.

True, it sprayed Indian Ink indiscriminately onto the stencils and the stencillers, but after some practice Mrs Verrall and her stalwart helpers mastered it and were soon beginning to churn out answers to the heaps of letters the Post Office dumped obligingly on the wooden floor of the pavilion. They worked out a system. Stella Verrall, armed with a stapler and a paper-knife of menacing sharpness, tackled the envelopes. A quick slit with the knife under the flap of the envelope, a quick bang on the stapler to fasten the enclosed cheque (if any) to its letter, and the letter went one way, the envelope another. At the table to her left, Araminta Simpson quickly snipped the stamps off the envelopes, which she then discarded. ('You'll make quite a bit out of the stamps,' Lady Elizabeth advised.) On Mrs Verrall's right, Gauvinier sorted the letters into four piles: the first, and largest, was the 'thank you for your support' pile; the second, smaller but still significantly bulky, was 'thank you for your support and donation of . . .' pile; third came 'cricket clubs'; and fourth combined the second and third categories and any that Gauvinier wanted to think about answering. Any insulting communications were dropped into a wastepaper basket labelled 'rubbish', not for destruction but for counting later.

Gauvinier had composed *pro forma* letters for categories one to three, and Arabella Simpson (it was her day off) and Rose Hunter, each with piles of stencilled letters, folded, inserted, licked and stamped envelopes at quite astonishing speed. The pile on the 'For posting' table grew apace. In mid-afternoon Polly turned up with a large basket of sandwiches and two flasks of coffee, and the weary workers were refreshing themselves when a discreet knocking at the door proclaimed the arrival of BBC's Nationwide team.

A balding man in a grey-blue business suit of impeccable cut put his head round the door apologetically, homed in on Gauvinier with the ease born of long practice, and offered a limp hand.

'Mr Gauvinier, I presume?'

Gauvinier resisted the urge to reply in appropriate fashion, but contented himself with a nod.

'My name's McLean. Producer, BBC Nationwide. I believe you're expecting us?'

'Oh yes, your people rang me this morning. D'you want me now?'

'Well, if we could just set up for the interview, it would be very helpful.'

'Why not? Where do you want me? How soon will you be ready?'

'Not to worry, we won't disturb you. I'll just get the chaps in.'

'Oh.' A little blankly, Gauvinier watched as McLean called from the doorway: 'OK, Fred. You can get the blokes in now.'

A burly man with short, crinkly grey hair came in, carrying a clip-board. He cast about him with an expert eye, made a few notes and went out again.

McLean, somewhat effusively, shook Gauvinier by the hand again.

'Good-bye, old chap. If you have any bother, Fred's your man. I must go and survey the ground for next Sunday. Ta-ta.'

'Wait a minute. Next Sunday? What's all that about?'

'Oh, didn't anyone tell you? We're putting out your next match, live on Two. There's some hitch about the John Player League – contract up to maggots I expect – so we're filling in with your little lot. 'Bye.' He drew the last word out to at least three times its normal length and, with a languid wave of the hand, was gone. Gauvinier never saw him again, except as a shadowy figure disappearing behind a large van painted dark green, with 'BBC Outside Broadcasts' in discreet gold lettering on the side.

It was parked under the chestnut trees, its roof brushing the dark green leaves aside. There were two more vans there, and four private cars. As Gauvinier stared, Fred came stumping back, followed by four men carrying equipment.

'What's all this?' Gauvinier asked impatiently.

'Lights.'

Suddenly, the quiet recreation ground seemed a hive of activity. Two men were running up a latticed aerial with a round disc on top, from the back of a flat-backed truck. Four others ran out long cables from the lorry. One was on the pavilion roof, feeding more cables down through a skylight.

'Linesmen.' Fred's communication was monosyllabic.

An exquisite young man with a multi-coloured scarf, purple corduroy jeans and dark sunglasses joined them.

'We'll need at least four mikes inside, Fred, please dear. And we'll need two sixes *and* the eight. I've told that darling man Eustace. He was mumbling something about the power supply – Oh, Christ that's what he meant.' There was a muddled flash and a muted explosion from somewhere within the pavilion and all the lights went out.

'I *knew* we'd overload the system. What a bore. We'll have to bring a line in from somewhere else. *What* a bore! Be a dear, then, Fred, and fix it up, won't you?' He ran a flaccid hand across his brow and noticed Gauvinier. 'Who're you? Oh, I say. The sparks'll fix it all up in just a jiff. Nothing to worry about. I'm Monty. Director, you know.'

'Perhaps you'd be good enough to let me know what's happening. It's like being overrun by a swarm of locusts.'

Monty laughed out loud.

'Oh, you are a one!' Gauvinier had always believed this particular line belonged to a particular breed of comedian. 'Yes, I suppose we are rather much, when you come to think of it.'

The pavilion, which on Saturday and Sunday afternoons seemed perfectly adequate to house twenty-two players, two umpires, two scorers, the President and his wife, two tea ladies and sundry friends and relations, now seemed half buried under the avalanche of equipment and personnel which had taken it over. Gauvinier counted thirty different bodies, each apparently fully occupied, busily engaged on wiring up, powering up, laying out, lighting and preparing for filming what had apparently become a television studio. He and his helpers felt superfluous.

Every piece of equipment seemed to have its own technician. Some, like the expensive looking camera, had two humans to care for it. In addition, each camera, lighting bank, cable roll and microphone, to Gauvinier's dazzled eyes, had two more men to unpack it, carry it, set it up and reverse the process afterwards.

'Monty' took one look inside the pavilion, wrinkled a sensitive nose and murmured: 'This won't do. This won't do at all,' and ordered everyone outside, Mrs Verrall and helpers included. As the lights had not yet been fixed, there was little they could do anyway, and they seemed fascinated by the spectacle of one of Britain's greatest institutions, the BBC, in full spate. 'It's better than the films,' 'Minta whispered to 'Bella. After an hour the scene was reminiscent of the annual visit of the circus. Bobby Bewers led eighteen boys of the choir straight from practice and still in their cassocks to cheer on the proceedings. Cables littered the ground. The aerial towered twenty feet above the chestnuts like the mast of a battleship, and the inside of the pavilion, flooded with brilliant light, was totally transformed.

A girl with a long jaw and determined eyes introduced herself to Gauvinier as 'Helen the floor manager'. He had some difficulty in understanding her, and in making her understand him, as she spoke to him through a piece of electronic wizardry which encircled her throat and seemed ready to gag her whenever she opened her mouth to speak. It was attached to a huge pair of ear muffs, from which a cable ran out of the pavilion into the mists which were beginning to gather. After some misunderstanding, Helen the floor manager cajoled him, with a series of waves, to accept a tiny microphone pinned to his shirt. He had the most curious sensation as a waft of Chanel No. 5 hit his senses and a girl sound technician shoved one hand up his trousers and another down them to wire him up with expertise and the ghost of a wink in baby blue eyes. She moved behind him. He was just becoming accustomed to her poking her finger into his ear when he realized suddenly that he could hear what was going on. It was not a finger in his ear: it was an ear-piece. Fingers pressed on a piece of sticky plaster to hold the wire down to his neck.

'Good-oh,' came Monty's voice, loud and clear. 'Interviewee's got sound now. Is your deaf-aid comfortable, dear?'

Gauvinier understood from Helen the floor manager that this referred to him. He nodded.

'Speak to me. Oh dear God, speak to me.'

The floor manager's voice cut in.

'Say something to him. You've got a mike now.'

'Who, me?'

'Yes, go on,' she added encouragingly. 'It won't bite.'

'I can hear you,' said Gauvinier, keeping his head, and promptly heard himself echoing almost simultaneously in the earpiece. It sounded like 'I – ca – I – nhe – ca – nhear – you – raryou – you.'

'Oh, Christ, he's got bloody feed-back. Sound. Jesus Christ, sound. For Pete's sake clear the bloody system – we're – on – the – air – in – five – minutes – well, three hours anyway.'

Another voice broke in. Cool, clear, girlish.

'Five minutes to rehearsal. Camera one, ready. Camera two, ready. Camera three. Are you ready yet?'

'Hold it love. Something up to maggots with this bloody antic.'

The floor manager cut in again.

'It doesn't matter for a bit. Johnnie isn't here yet.'

'Oh for Christ's sake.' It was Monty's favourite remark. 'Bloody editorial again. Where's he gone this time? I thought he was supposed to be here with the producer. Where's McLean?'

'Don't worry, Peter,' the floor manager called everyone by his Christian name. 'It'll be all right on the night. Oh, lor'.' She clicked a switch and spoke into her microphone. 'Monty, where the hell's the monitor?'

'How the hell should I know? That's your job.'

'But you promised to get an authorization for a colour monitor. What the hell's the use of a B/W picture in this day and age?'

A new voice cut in.

'All right everybody. Ten minutes.'

There was a click. All sound died in Gauvinier's ears, the brilliant lights faded quite slowly, and he was left blinking in the now half-gloom of the pavilion's three bulbs.

'Time for tea,' said Helen the floor manager. 'Don't worry. We'll just unplug you.'

'But I thought she said five minutes to rehearsal.'

'Oh, don't worry your little head about a thing like that. Someone gave her a time way back and that's the only thing she can do, is to count down to it. Anyway, Johnny Preece isn't here yet so we can't start. Come and have a cup of tea.' Gauvinier realized that one of the vans was a well-equipped canteen. He was handed a steaming mug, then a voice in his ear said: 'Excuse me, Mr Gauvinier.'

A youngish man with a half-familiar face held out a hand.

'My name's Foster. Southern TV. I rang you. Can you spare us five minutes for a quickie? This mob'll be hours, yet, and if we slip in now while they're having tea we'll make the six o'clock.'

Gauvinier looked around. Nobody was taking any notice. The entire BBC crew were lounging about, smoking, sipping their tea. There was no reason why he could not take a few minutes.

'Sure you'll be quick, Mr Foster?' he asked the young man.

'Got the crew right here. Let's just take a level and we're off. OK, Len.'

Gauvinier saw a cameraman hoist his camera on to his shoulder. Beside him a second man in a duffle coat stood, headphones over ears. A third man stood, arm raised. A brilliant light flooded Gauvinier, and Foster held a bulbous grey microphone towards him, covered in nylon sponge.

'Tell me, Mr Gauvinier, what did you have for breakfast?'

Surprised, Gauvinier answered, 'Kellogg's Cornflakes and a boiled egg, toast and ——'

'That's fine. OK, Bill?'

The soundman nodded. 'Go ahead.'

'Tell me, Mr Gauvinier, why do you object to the Superstores scheme?'

'Well, in the first place it's going to mean the end of Tillingfold Cricket Club, on this ground, at least. And it will mean the end of the village as we know it.' (Keep your answers short, but not too short, Renton had said.)

'But you've been promised alternative grounds. Why can't you just move and play elsewhere?'

'On the surface that's the simple answer. But when you've

been playing on the same ground for – well, 150 years if not twice that – there's much more to it than just tradition. In many ways I can't explain why, but I'm convinced that Tillingfold represents a great deal of the best in England, and many of us here are willing to fight for it.'

'But don't you think that in today's values, cricket is an old-fashioned, slow, out-of-date game?'

'Only to those who don't have the intelligence to appreciate something good,' said Gauvinier sharply. (Watch it, he said to himself. Don't lose your cool.)

'So you rate everyone who doesn't like cricket unintelligent?'

(This young man was quick. Gauvinier knew he had made a mistake.)

'Not at all. But I happen to believe that the world has destroyed far too much that is good in the name of progress without replacing it with anything better.'

'Do you think cricket is in danger of being destroyed?'

'In one way cricket is stronger than it has been since the turn of the century, in the so-called golden years of W. G. Grace. There's more interest and more money in it, largely thanks to Kerry Packer, whom I happen to have some time for. But – and this is where I part company with Packer – it is in danger because in modernizing the game we stand the risk of damaging its essential character. No, there's no threat to cricket itself in Tillingfold; that will carry on no matter what Sir Philip Beeston does with his Superstores.'

'Thank you Mr Gauvinier.' A pause. The interview was over. 'That's a very nice piece. You won't mind if I do the cutaway?'

Gauvinier watched intrigued as the reporter posed again for his cameraman, in a different position this time, and repeated the questions to the camera. He explained how this would simplify the film editor's task should the interview have to be shortened. With sound-on-film it was necessary for the editor to be able to insert questions at apposite places in order to avoid the professional's anathema – a 'jump-cut'.

'Cheerio.' The young man grinned. 'Good luck with the Beeb.

Don't let them drown you.' The whole incident had taken ten minutes, and now the BBC's floor manager was hovering agitatedly, a sound engineer was poised with a neck-mike at the end of a long piece of wire, and lights were flooding from the pavilion windows.

Gauvinier saw what he meant. Technicians, equipment, cameramen, lights and vans merged into a scenario that quite overwhelmed Tillingfold's modest pavilion. An hour or so later:

'There's been a change of plan,' announced the floor manager. 'Don't worry, it makes it easier. The editorial aren't coming down after all. Johnny Preece will be interviewing you from the studio. We'll put a monitor under the camera and he'll ask you the questions. You'll hear him through the ear-piece, of course, otherwise there'd be feed-back.'

Gauvinier, suitably wired for sound, hair combed to a semblance of respectability, was alternately patted and shoved into his chair behind a table piled with letters, opened and unopened. He sighed, realizing that the sorting would have to begin again.

'Who's going to be interviewing me?' he asked the girl.

'Oh, I don't know, Preece or one of that mob. He at least knows a bit about cricket. By rights it should be Bough, but they'll probably give the job to one of the girls who doesn't know a cricket bat from a hole in the ground.'

'Two minutes,' said a voice in his ear. Then Monty's high voice, overriding the din. 'Don't worry, old boy, just watch the monitor screen, there in front of you.'

Gauvinier peered forward. By straining over the top of the pile of letters, he could just see the screen, under the camera lens which pointed towards him with the implacability of a gun muzzle.

'Shove that junk out of the way . . . That's right. Now you can see. Don't worry about a thing.'

Gauvinier saw the languid figure of Johnny Preece in the monitor screen, sinking languidly into a chair. He carried a clipboard, which he consulted with a faint air of boredom.

'Thirty seconds to programme.' A girl's voice cut in on the talk-back.

'Fifteen seconds . . .'

'Quiet everybody. *On* air in ten seconds.' Monty's voice.

The background babble in Gauvinier's ear-piece hushed as the clear feminine voice counted down from ten to zero. Nothing happened. Preece sprawled ungainly in his chair. Gauvinier cast desperate eyes towards the floor manager, who raised her expressive eyebrows and opened her hands in exasperated impotence.

Suddenly Preece shot upright, straightened his tie, coughed and said, 'Sorry about that' in his nice apologetic way, stared straight out of the monitor set at Gauvinier and intoned, slowly gathering confidence:

'Well, after a little hiccough we come to the story of Tillingfold, the cricket club that may turn into a complex of department stores in the heart of rural Sussex. It seems that Superstores, the multi-million pound company owned by Sir Philip Beeston, the well-known tycoon, plan to plant seven acres of everything from baked beans to baby food, right on the cricket pitch.

'Some say that this will bring progress and prosperity to a neglected part of rural Sussex. Others won't be dragged, kicking and screaming, into the twentieth century. Among them is Peter Gauvinier, captain of the local cricket club. I'm going to talk to him now, live, in the pavilion of Tillingfold Cricket Club.'

His voice lifted slightly, as in hope, towards the end of the last sentence. For a second or two nothing happened, then, as Preece began to speak again, the picture on the screen changed, and Gauvinier suddenly saw himself, absurdly small behind a table packed with envelopes.

'Oh well, there you are. Good evening, Mr Gauvinier, or may I call you Peter?'

Preece was always polite. It was part of his charm.

'Yes, of course. Can I call you Johnny?'

'Help yourself, old boy. Certainly, Peter. Well, we won't bother about that. What I want to know is, er, what is that great pile of letters you have there?'

Gauvinier looked about him. A slight feeling of helplessness came over him. 'They're letters from people who've been writing to us in support of our efforts to save Tillingfold cricket ground,' he said.

'That's – er – wonderful, er, Peter, isn't it? Would you like to open one for us now – any one you like, and read us what it says?'

'All right.'

Gauvinier plunged his hand into the pile and came out with a plain envelope. He slipped his forefinger under the flap and ripped it open. A cheque was pinned to a typewritten note.

As he scanned the note his jaw dropped in astonishment, and nationwide the audience heard him exclaim:

'Good God!'

Unfortunately, the cause of his astonishment was not revealed to an expectant public. For simultaneously, with that exquisite sense of timing for which he was renowned, Preece coughed apologetically and cut in.

'Er, huh, er, huh-huh. I'm afraid that's all we've time for now. Fascinating story. Fascinating. Now for the weather news – '

'Sorry, Mr Gauvinier,' Monty's voice sounded close in his ear. 'The darlings often do that on us.'

Gauvinier hardly heard him. He was still staring at the note in his hand.

> 'Dear Mr Gauvinier, I am sorry not to have been able to see you on Saturday evening. I understand that my son explained the situation to you. He is a difficult young man to get to know and I must congratulate you. He does not usually take so kindly to strangers.
>
> 'Without going into details I can reassure you about Tillingfold CC and its ground. My company's strategic plan for the future certainly contained Tillingfold as a key factor, perhaps not entirely as presented to the public. However, the publicity has created such an adverse reaction to the original plan that we feel obliged to re-orientate our thinking to some degree. The whole affair has, however, clarified our perspective, and for this we are grateful.
>
> 'Your club has no doubt been put to some expense in this

matter, and this quite rightly should be borne by Superstores. I therefore enclose a cheque for £1,000 to cover your disbursements, and would request you to put the residue, if any, towards the re-surfacing of your square. When I inspected it the other evening I noticed a disturbing absence of "body" in the turf and the very dusty nature of the topsoil.

'With best wishes,

'Philip Beeston.

'P.S. Perhaps we could arrange a yearly fixture between Tillingfold and Ashley-on-Thames.'

'So Nationwide missed a scoop?' Oliver Fanshawe laughed until he coughed and the tears sprang from his eyes. 'There was I, absolutely livid about what they'd done to you, and you were sitting there holding the best story of the year by a long chalk. Still, it gave Renton something to crow about.'

'Indeed it has. He's sent the whole thing off to the *Bugle*, and the rest of Fleet Street is besieging him for information. He's done three radio interviews already. It's like a lot of hungry dogs after scraps of meat. Still, he's got plenty of them. Just so long as he doesn't come worrying us.'

Gauvinier had taken flight from the Press and broadcasting the moment the contents of Beeston's letter had sunk in. In the hour of victory he did not wish to crow. More, he felt anti-climax in that all the plans he had been making would now have to be dropped. There would be no sit-down at the Lord's Test match. He would not lead a thousand flannel-clad warriors on an assault of the Ministry of Environment. There would be no march to London, playing the great clubs on the way. The grand gesture had not been made by Tillingfold; in defeat, Beeston had upstaged them with his cash and his easy flow of words. He laughed suddenly.

Fanshawe looked at him closely and signalled the barman. They had driven in his three-wheeler out over the Downs and down to a little inn in the country near Horsham, ten miles away. No one would find them there and they were unrecognized.

'Don't worry, Peter. You've won. *Won*. Now all you've got to do is to spend the money. Or we have. How much is there.'

'With Beeston's thousand, there's around £1,700, and more to come. It's all turned out rather well. We'll be able to re-lay the square and to tart up the pavilion as well. I think we could afford to lay on a really good dinner dance at Christmas, too – subsidize it, you know. It would be good for the club. But that's up to the committee.'

'Good idea. But you've still got a few fences to mend, you know. There's James; and Fred 'n' Frank. And young Trine's had his nose put out of joint a bit.'

'I think James Mitterman began his rehabilitation last Sunday.'

'You mean his innings? I never thought he had it in him.'

Gauvinier nodded. ''The others are merely suffering from dented prospects and they'll soon come round. Fred Bason was horribly guilty anyway, and Frank would be fine if he'd get his accounts in order. I believe Mitterman's offered to do something there to help. As for Teddy, well, it's all water off a duck's back to him. If he went off Beachy Head he'd fall on to a luxury yacht with a blonde sunning herself on a Lilo.'

Fanshawe laughed with genuine affection.

'They're not a bad side, are they? But there's one thing still puzzling me. Just why did Beeston pull out like that? D'you think he was frightened off by the publicity? He's had plenty of that for years and it's never worried him before. Or d'you think it's just because he loves cricket? Surely that young devil of a son couldn't have that much influence on him.'

'I don't know either,' Gauvinier replied slowly. 'Perhaps we'll never know. Mitterman won't talk, that's for sure. Like one for the road?'

'Not for me, I'm driving. Don't let me stop you. In fact, make it a double. You can drink mine as well. After all, you've got quite a lot to celebrate.'

'Yes,' said Gauvinier reflectively. 'Right. I will.' He shook his head, as if clearing it, and grinned broadly at Fanshawe.

'At least I won't lie awake worrying tonight. Oliver, d'you think I should resign? It's time someone else took over.'

'Not on your life, Peter. You don't want to, do you?'

'Not really. But I have had a long innings, you know. And I keep wondering what's going to hit us next. I'm getting a bit old for this sort of thing.'

Chapter 10

'Good morning, sir. My name is Death.'

Gauvinier, considerably startled, stepped back a pace, which brought him into painful contact with his own front door.

'I beg your pardon?'

'Death, sir. Inspector Death of Billington CID. My name. Sorry to startle you. It sometimes has that effect on people.'

Gauvinier, whose contact with Her Majesty's Police Force consisted of an occasional pint with the rustically named Sergeant Pippin in the skittle bar of the Dog and Duck, studied the proffered identity card with a degree of vagueness unusual to him. He remembered his manners.

'Come in, Inspector. Would you like some coffee? My wife isn't at home, but if you don't mind the kitchen? . . .'

'Very kind, I must say, sir.'

Inspector Death followed Gauvinier into the kitchen, bright with blue and white chequered curtains and sunlight. He was small and neat, like a small brown mouse, thought Gauvinier. Brown suit, well pressed, brown shirt and tie; brown leather shoes, worn but polished to a deep ruddy shine. He carried a brown brief-case.

His voice was nondescript, unidentifiable. Gauvinier thought that in a crowd he would be easily lost. Sitting in his kitchen, sipping his coffee, Gauvinier thought Inspector Death looked like the man they sent to perform routine tasks, to compile the dossiers. He looked young for a Detective-Inspector, though.

Gauvinier, busying himself with kettle, milk, Nescafé and sugar, made small talk.

'That's an odd name for a policeman. Couldn't you, well, change it?'

The cool brown eyes looked at him.

'No odder than Plant the gardener, or Smith the smith. My father called himself De'Ath, but then he was a removal specialist and Death Removals might have been a little suggestive.' He grinned and Gauvinier decided he was human after all.

'What can I do for you, Inspector?' he asked, pouring boiling water.

Detective-Inspector Death paused, as if to compose his thoughts. Eventually he drew a slight but audible breath and launched into rapid, but carefully constructed speech. It was as though he had learned it by heart. It sounded rather pompous.

'I am instructed to inform you that what I have to say is highly confidential and touches on many very delicate matters,' he began. 'My superiors would be most grateful if you would treat what I am about to say as confidential. Highly confidential.' He paused and looked inquiringly at Gauvinier. On Gauvinier's nod, he continued. 'With one exception, I am unable to mention any names to you. In fact it will be wiser but no doubt you will be able to put two and two together. However, we would be grateful if you do not make public the results of any speculation in which you may indulge.'

'All right,' said Gauvinier, handing him a steaming mug. 'You can come off your high horse. I won't talk.'

'Good,' said Inspector Death, slightly less formally. 'You may as well know that I am acting under the direct orders of the Chief

Constable in this matter, and that he is doing what he is told on the instructions of Scotland Yard. Fraud Squad.'

'Beeston?' inquired Gauvinier.

'Sorry, no names,' replied the policeman. 'All I am authorized to say is that as a result of our inquiries certain parties will shortly be charged with committing a variety of offences, among them bribery, conspiracy to defraud, and fraud itself. I can't tell you any more, even though you know something of the story yourself.

'All I can tell you is that your club treasurer, James Mitterman, will *not* be among those charged. Whatever you may think of the circumstances surrounding this case, Mr Mitterman is in the clear.' He grinned his attractive grin again. 'You might say he smells as sweet as new-mown hay.'

'How are you going to shut Renton up? He knows all I do and perhaps a lot more. It was because of what he told me that I wrote to the Chief Constable.'

'Don't worry about Renton, sir. We can cope with him. He'd sell his soul *and* his grandmother for an exclusive and we've told him he can have a twelve-hour beat on the arrests in return for a little co-operation.'

'So this means the development scheme is off? Finished? Kaput?'

'Well, sir, I don't suppose you'll hear any more of that little lot. We'll be glad to get it all settled too. We've been waiting for fifteen years for some of these gentlemen.' He sounded smug.

'Did they fall, or were they pushed?' Gauvinier asked, suddenly suspicious. The inspector smiled thinly, stood up and put his coffee cup neatly on the draining board.

'I can't say any more now, sir. But you might owe a certain gentleman an apology. There are more courageous things to do than stopping a cricket ball. I'll find my own way out. Good morning.'

Gauvinier stared through the window after his retreating back. Maybe he did owe Mitterman an apology after all, for more things than one. But he still didn't have to like the man, did he? And now he would have to undo all his plans. The battle had fizzled out before it had begun. He felt deflated.

The following week, Tillingfold's nets were unusually busy – whether because of the publicity or out of goodwill, Gauvinier could not tell. There was a prickliness in the atmosphere, as though the cricketers did not wish to say anything that could be construed as out of place.

'Too damned polite by half,' he thought to himself as he strapped on his pads for the usual knock. Mitterman was there too, eager to join in and with everyone eager to ensure that he did so.

'After you, James.'

'No, no, it's your turn.'

'Oh well, OK. Oh, sorry . . .'

'Not at all. My fault. After you . . .'

'Would you like a decent ball, Mr Mitterman?'

'That's kind of you, Fred. There's no need – '

'Don't think another word of it, sir . . .'

Gauvinier, on his knees padding up, his back to the net, flinched involuntarily as Jess, batting, pulled a short ball very hard. It sang along the net, twanged against a guy rope, and there was a sudden cry of 'Look out' as it spun quite viciously over the top of the net towards a small group of onlookers.

They scattered hastily, except one, a girl. She caught the ball competently without hesitation or fear, and instead of throwing it back she strolled towards the nets, tossing it between her hands. As she approached, Gauvinier saw that she was dark, with curly short hair, crisp blue eyes and rosy cheeks. She was wearing a purple track suit and a college scarf. He had never seen her before in his life.

She looked down at him.

'D'you mind if I have a go?'

He looked at her, surprised.

'No, I don't suppose so. D'you want to have a bat?'

'No, just a bowl.'

'Well, you caught that well enough just now. And you're dressed for it.'

He glanced at her training shoes. They were scrubbed clean, and well worn.

'Can you play cricket?' he asked.

'A little,' replied the girl, flushing slightly. 'That's why I'd like to have a go.'

'I'd better warn the chaps,' said Gauvinier. 'They're not used to young ladies with sporting inclinations.'

'Here, fellows,' he called. 'This young lady wants to have a bowl.'

There was a chorus of gruff voices, a laugh or two, and a muted wolf whistle. Gauvinier made a mental note to have a word with Paul White later.

They stood back, awkwardly, to give her room. She paced out her run-up – ten paces, and turned.

'Give 'er stick, Albert,' a voice called; and down the net Albert Jess took firm guard. He had no idea what to expect – underarm, floater, a lobbed 'dolly-drop' – but he wasn't going to be bowled out by a mere girl.

'She looks as though she knows what she's doing,' Hunter breathed in Trine's ear.

'She'd better,' he grunted. 'Nice looker, though.'

The girl, aware of their all-male reactions, consciously made herself relax. She breathed deeply, dropped her shoulders, and set off on a rhythmic approach to the wicket. Her arm came over easily, smoothly, a little low for the purist perhaps, but the ball, aimed just outside the off-stump, swung in quite sharply and lifted off the damp turf, nipping behind Jess's hasty defensive prod and hitting him with a hollow thwack plumb in the box. He went down like a felled ox, the breath forced out of his lungs in an explosive 'Oooooh!'

The girl, heedless of the entire Tillingfold team, who stood mouths agape, unable to move, yelled, 'Oh my God, I'm sorry,' and ran quickly down the net to the stricken Jess who, surprised to find himself in one piece and actually not too much hurt, hastened to struggle to his feet. Competently she made him bend over to get his breath back and beckoned imperiously to Trine, who happened to be standing nearest.

'Here, you,' she said imperiously, 'Come and give him a rub. Well, I can't now, can I?'

Trine, galvanized, trotted down the pitch to help, followed by several of the others, eager to cover their embarrassment. The girl turned to Gauvinier, who knew suddenly that Nemesis, whom he thought he had avoided successfully in the person of Sir Philip Beeston, had turned up again wearing a St Catherine's scarf and American training shoes.

'Sorry about that,' she said matter-of-factly. 'But it was his own fault. He didn't get behind the line and that was a terrible shot. All right hand and cross-bat. D'you mind if I carry on? I'll try not to wound anyone too badly.'

'No, no. Sure. Help yourself.' Gauvinier felt flustered. 'I'm taking the knock now, myself. Do your worst.' He grinned and hurried to take his place at the wicket, Jess having been escorted, still looking shaken, to take his pads off and to examine the protective piece of plastic that had saved, if not quite his life, at least his person. Gauvinier felt that any girl as self-possessed as this one could well cope with a dozen embarrassed males, even on their own ground, and he was right. She was soon at home, taking her turn bowling to him, and he discovered that indeed she could more than merely 'bowl a bit'. She wasn't as fast as Norman Smith, but more accurate, and her faster ball was quicker than Bill Budgeon could manage. She kept quite a good length and varied her pace and her swing enough to require watching. He was impressed, and at the end of the net, said so.

'Thank you, kind sir.' She mocked him with the easy familiarity a pretty girl can get away with with an older man.

'My name's Peter Gauvinier. I'm Tillingfold's skipper,' he said. 'It's been a privilege to have you. May I know whom we have the honour of entertaining?'

'I'm Jill Grantham, and I hope you still think so when I've

said what I'm going to say,' she said flatly, looking at him with disconcertingly blue eyes.

Gauvinier, male ego rising, had to remind himself firmly that he was married and at least twice this remarkable girl's age.

'Go on,' he said, half jokingly, in that peculiarly condescending manner an older man can use to a pretty girl. 'Shock me.'

'Oh, I will,' said Jill Grantham. 'We've just moved into the village. I want to join the cricket club. As a player.'

Gauvinier became conscious that the cricketers, hearing the exchange, had left tidying up the net and were clustered round them. The girl was saying 'How much *is* the subscription?'

He heard Trine's voice: 'Five pounds a year if you're over eighteen. Two pounds if you're still a junior. We've never had a girl before. I don't know if you'd qualify for a reduced rate.'

'Oh no,' she said calmly. 'It's top whack or nothing.' Like a man, she fished in the back pocket of her tracksuit and brought out a crumpled five-pound note. 'Here you are, Mr Gauvinier. Here's the money.' She held it out to him.

'Go on, Guv, take it. It's real.' Edward Trine's voice was bantering.

Fred Bason and Frank Hunter spoke together.

'Wait a moment,' said Bason.

'Hang on a bit,' said Hunter.

They glared at one another. Gauvinier felt pressurized. A part of him said that he ought to accept the money as commonplace; another felt the absurdity of the situation – 'fancy a girl wanting to play cricket' was the phrase that sprang to his mind even as he rejected it. Strangely, it was Mitterman who relieved his embarrassment. He leaned over between Frank 'n' Fred and plucked the note from Gauvinier's hesitant fingers.

'Thank you, Peter, I'll take that, as treasurer.' Somehow he produced a thin notebook. 'What is your full name, Miss, er Grantham is it? I'll send you a receipt. My name's Mitterman. James Mitterman, Secretary-Treasurer.'

'Thank you Mr. Mitterman. Yes, that's right. Gillian Grantham.'

She breathed deeply. Making history was an effort.

'Hold it there, everybody.'

There was a brilliant flash. Renton stood a few paces away, his face hidden by a Nikon camera, with a little square flash pack on top. 'Once more.'

The flash winked again.

'Thanks everyone. Just what we needed.'

Gauvinier recognized with a sinking feeling that Renton was right. Miss Grantham would be a gift from the gods for the publicity man, though what good it would do Tillingfold he could not see. Renton expressed his thoughts in the old dictum of the agency man:

'There's no such thing as bad publicity. Don't look so down, Guv.'

The familiarity infuriated Gauvinier, but he said nothing. Gillian put her hand on his arm. Compared with her earlier aplomb, she seemed embarrassed.

'I really didn't do it for that, Mr Gauvinier. Really I didn't.'

Gauvinier believed her, looked at her and was lost. He was as susceptible as the next man to a pair of blue eyes and a slim figure. 'I know you didn't – ' He nearly said, 'my dear' but coughed instead. Patronizing would only make things worse.

'Whether you meant it or not, you're getting it. In any case,' he added with some vigour, trying to reassert his control of the situation, 'we don't know yet whether you *can* join the club. We'll have to hold a special meeting.' It was in his mind that several things might be resolved at one time. There was nothing like a good shake-up to sort things out.

'Ay, ah think tha's best.' Frank Hunter had been holding himself back with difficulty. 'It's all very well letting a girl have a go in nets, but she can't come and *play.*' He put enormous emphasis on the word 'play'. 'You can't have a girl in dressing-room while you're putting on your box.'

''Ear, 'ear.' Fred Bason rumbled assent. 'Wouldn't be right, miss, y'see. You wouldn't like what goes on in a men's dressing-room. There's the language, for one thing. Not right for a girl's ears.'

'That's right,' Paul White broke in. 'He farts. Particularly after a couple of pints at dinner time.' There was a circle of guffaws.

'That's enough.' Gauvinier was always annoyed by deliberate gaucherie. But the girl stood her ground, flushing slightly.

'It'll take more than that to bowl this maiden over.'

'You don't know old Fred's farts.'

But this time the offensive edge was missing from the crude words, and the laughter genuine. The girl joined in.

Gauvinier broke it up.

'Come along everyone, let's get the nets away. I'm getting thirsty. Gillian, you take the guy ropes off. Fred, take that pole. Frank, get the pegs up. And Albert, if you're fit again, pack up the bag and make sure it's all correct. Then we'll all go down to the pub for a quick one. We've got something to celebrate today.'

'Some girl, that,' Jess paused from packing the pads into the big leather bag and grinned up at him. 'I've been smitten before, but never by a cricket ball in the crutch. As an introduction, I don't recommend it.'

Gauvinier watched the figures rolling up the netting in the darkening dusk. In her track suit and shoes Gillian was indistinguishable from the men.

'Do you think they'll accept her?' he said slowly. Beside him Fanshawe sighed heavily.

'It's not up to us, you know, Peter. But I don't think cricket will ever be the same again.'